FAILURE
AS A WAY OF
LIFE

ATLATL

Atlatl Press
POB 293161
Dayton, Ohio 45429
atlatlpress.com

Also by Andersen Prunty

FAILURE

AS A WAY OF

LIFE

To Failure!
Why not?

1
A Failure's Failure

GUS'S PANTS ARE down around his ankles, his large pale buttocks hovering over the open well. Using his phone, I take a photo of him, sure to get the sign in frame.

The sign reads:

NO FOREIGN OBJECTS ARE TO BE ADMITTED INTO THE
WELL OF PURITY

It's dark outside and the sign is hard to read and Gus is hard to see and this was probably a terrible idea to begin with. I'm just glad the phone is in my face, putting at least a layer of glass and circuitry and metal in between my eyes and the chubby middle-aged man squatting over the well. Watching other guys shit isn't normally my thing. I usually even turn my head when animals do it. Maybe I'm scat averse.

Gus and I both work for a company called Dr. Jolly's Godwater and have for the past decade or so. It's in a small hippie college town a few miles north of Dayton called Twin Springs. Neither one of us has gotten a raise the entire time we've been there but the job is beyond easy and there is a sliver of health benefits I need for my kid. I don't really need them for myself since I never go to the doctor. Even though I probably should. Especially with this rash.

Anyway, this lack of a raise is the reason for Gus's current compromised position. It's also the reason neither one of us has shaved or cut his hair in a really long time. It's why we both wear the same clothes to work every day. It's probably why we both smell really bad.

"I can't do it," he grunts. I'm not sure why he grunts. It's like he's trying to convince me.

"What do you mean you can't do it?" I lower his phone and focus on the sign so I don't have to look at him.

"I must be constipated or something."

"It's because you eat too much fucking meat. I thought you said you went at this time every day. Like clockwork, you said."

"Well, I can't. I'm not going to force myself. That's harmful. Plus my legs are getting tired."

"Come on then. We can try again some other time. Maybe bring an enema."

"Fuck that." He stands and pulls up his pants. "You could do it."

"No fucking way. I'm not shitting in front of you."

"I don't have to take a picture. I don't even have to be around."

"I went earlier. I don't have to. I guess you could just piss into it."

"Yeah." Gus looks really excited. "Why didn't I think of that?"

He stands in position, tugging his penis out of his underwear and aiming for the well.

I hold the phone back up to my face and think, not for the first time, that we're probably too old to be doing this.

He starts pissing and a sudden breeze sweeps through, throwing Gus's urine back onto him. He quickly spins around while I quickly back far away from him and he continues pissing in the opposite direction, toward me.

"Maybe it just wasn't meant to be." I grab a handful of grass from around the well and chuck it toward the opening, missing.

Gus shakes himself off and zips up. "Maybe it's protected or something."

10

I'm not religious or even very superstitious so I just say, "It's just fucking dirt water for rich people."

"You wanna go get some dinner?"

"Nah. I'm broke until we get paid again. Besides, Alice's probably wondering where I am." That probably isn't true at all, but just saying it makes me feel like she cares. "I think she's making Hamburger Helper." This probably is true and makes me sad.

Gus usually clams up at the mention of Alice. He's met her before and probably finds her attractive, as most guys seem to. I know I'm way out of my league and this doesn't help my anxiety surrounding the relationship. We met at the job. She only lasted about a week. She moved in with me after a month, I'm assuming because she hated her parents and I took her abuse. Also she probably has really low self-esteem. I wonder if Gus has ever jerked off to Alice online. He knows what she does. I wonder if he's ever sought her out. What does it matter? Why should Gus be different than any of the other countless guys Alice has and continues to 'entertain'? I'm sure he's at least used her as mental porn. Somehow this seems more flattering and less like my good friend and girlfriend are fucking (albeit in a virtual, non-physical way) behind my back and laughing about me the entire time.

We walk through a dewy, moonlit field to our cars, parked on a backcountry road.

"All right then. See you Monday," Gus says.

"See ya."

We both get into our cheap cars and start them up. Gus's is actually a small pick-up truck covered in dents and various shades of paint. His truck makes a low rumble and a burst of black smoke explodes from the tailpipe. The rear window is plastic. Mine is a small, cheap American car and when I start it, it makes a whiney noise like something is about to fly off and go into orbit. We'll both be pretty lucky to make it home.

2
Disaster Magic

It feels like the world is winding down. I recently turned forty. I've failed as a husband, failed as a father, failed as a child, failed as a writer, and am in the process of failing as a boyfriend. I've pretty much failed at being a human. There are a million ways to fail. I seem committed to exploring them all.

Over the winter I rented a house in Dayton with my girlfriend, Alice. It's the last house on a dead end street of a dying neighborhood in a dying city. I have five dead novels and over a hundred dead stories sitting in a Rubbermaid container in the attic. The plan is to drag them outside and burn them soon but I'll probably be too lazy to do that.

We've been here for a few months. It's a struggle to pay the monthly bills and I'm dreading the prospect of moving in with my dad. At least we have that option. Still, I feel tired and dry and know I should hope for something to give, some floodgate to open, but know no positive result could possibly come from that.

I sit in a chair in the living room drinking a beer I probably can't afford and staring at my bank account online, wondering how I'm going to come up with the car payment this month. Alice is in the bedroom working so I have to keep earbuds in to shut her out. I'm not a jealous guy or anything. It isn't even what she says to the 'client.' It's all online so it seems kind of imaginary. It's the fact that she says the same things to me during our rapidly decreasing sexual encounters. To the point I've had to ask her to please not say anything.

I raise my shirtsleeve to scratch an insanity-inducing itch. I notice a bloody patch of skin before digging in. I've had this rash for the past couple of weeks. When lying in bed at night, it feels like bugs are burrowing into my skin. The rash is definitely getting worse. Great, I think, now my body's failing.

My phone vibrates in my pocket and the usual burst of anxiety explodes in my chest and rockets to all of my nerve endings.

Nerves, I tell myself. That's what's causing the rash. I have to self-diagnose because I can't afford to go to a doctor, despite the insurance. Can't afford the copay. Probably wouldn't go anyway. My general rule is that I only go to the doctor if I black out, go blind, shit or piss blood, or have a pain in the same area for over a month. Like, a constant pain. Not one that comes and goes. I consider myself fortunate none of these things have happened yet.

I pull my phone from my pocket and look at the screen.

UNKNOWN NUMBER

I accept the call, knowing as I bring it to my ear it will either be a wrong number or something terrible has happened to a family member. I close my eyes and hope what comes out of the phone isn't something that will detonate my world.

"Hello?" I hope the panic doesn't make my voice quaver.

Nothing comes out of the phone.

Or, at least, no words come out of the phone.

I imagine the place on the other side of the phone call.

There's an ocean view. Somewhere on the West Coast where it might still be daylight. The soft hiss of a gentle rain. A person—possibly female—holding the phone to soft lips. I have trouble envisioning anything other than the lips and chin, maybe a small hand gently gripping the phone. I won't let myself see anything more than this.

13

She breathes softly, almost inaudibly. And in the distance, the rain sinking into the ocean.

I don't know how long I sit there, taking in this vision, suppressing the caller's face, suppressing her name.

I open my eyes and bring the phone away from my head and look at the screen and notice there is no one on the other line. I check the call log. There's no record of an unknown number. It's entirely possible my brain is failing as well. I think about looking online to see if brain tumors can cause a rash.

From the bedroom, I hear Alice say, "You want me to get down on my knees and milk that thing, baby?"

I close my eyes and lean back in my chair and take a deep breath.

If she ever calls me baby, we'll have to break up. That's all there is to it.

I think about what I'm going to do. It's pretty much how I've spent my alone time the last fifteen years or so. Maybe longer. Like some light bulb is going to go off and I'm going to have an a-ha moment.

It doesn't seem like I have a lot of options left. Rather than getting old or sad or bitter or angry I need to accept that the rest of my life is going to be a disaster and manage to find the magic in that.

After all, how egotistical is it to think I deserve a good life? And besides, isn't that all subjective anyway? Who's to say I don't have a good life?

I have a house (for now).

I have a lovely girlfriend (for now).

My son is in good health.

Gus and I have been best friends since we were twelve, so I can't really imagine him going anywhere.

Dad's still alive.

Shouldn't I have gratitude for all this?

Is that what people mean when they use the term mindfulness? Being mindful about what we're doing and what we have?

So what if I don't get what I want?

Does anyone?

Do I even know what I want anymore?

If I had what I wanted, wouldn't I just want more?

My mind drifts back to the caller and the faraway place.

Sometimes I think I want to be anywhere but where I am now.

But I've probably always thought that, no matter where I was. It's lunacy to think that will change.

I plow the back of my hand with fingernails that really need trimming.

Failing continuously allows me to avoid stagnation. This rash is something new and different, potentially awful. But maybe not. It'll probably clear up on its own. Or maybe I'll have to go to the doctor and he'll look at it and find some other potentially life threatening but easily curable condition and he'll say, "It's a good thing you had that rash or we wouldn't have found out about your terrible life threatening condition. Now we can get it nipped in the bud." And maybe my recovery will be miraculous and the years of fog that have wrapped my brain will suddenly lift and I'll see everything clearly and appreciate everything more and realize my life has only been so difficult because I didn't know who I truly was and now, having that knowledge, the rest of my life will be a propulsive, forever forward flowing path filled with passion and conviction and satisfaction.

This is the beauty of disaster magic.

3
Viva Misanthropy

I PULL UP to the curb in front of our house and get out of my car. I never bother locking it anymore, even though our neighborhood isn't that great. If I lock it, it just means they'll break out the windows to get whatever it is they could possibly want from the inside. I can live without the stereo or the loose change in the console. I don't really want to deal with a broken window. Maybe it's a pride thing.

I smell something burning and think maybe one of our neighbors is having a trash fire. I unlock the front door and step into the small house. The bedroom door is ajar. I listen for Alice to see if she's working.

I don't hear her.

I open the bedroom door and peek in.

The bed is messy but Alice isn't in it.

She has to be here somewhere. She hardly ever leaves.

I cover the rest of the house in a few seconds and still don't turn up any sign of her. I go into the kitchen and glance out the window into the backyard.

There she is.

Standing in front of the tiny charcoal grill, wearing a black bra, tiny athletic shorts, and combat boots. A sizeable flame lashes out from the grill.

Even though I find her increasingly difficult to be around, I still like looking at Alice, even though I have a sneaking suspicion she's a stand-in for someone else. She's a few inches shorter than me, slender, her short hair died black and sticking up wildly around her head. Not to mention that she's about fifteen years younger than me. Christ, what was I thinking? I should have known she would be too much to handle the first time I saw her. More importantly, what mental defect does she have that made her want to move in with me?

Since she seems preoccupied, I think about masturbating to her from the window. It's been at least a week since we've had sex. Her job understandably lowers her sex drive (at least with an actual physical partner, i.e. me) and I'm mostly depressed out of my skull nearly all the time. At least, that's the excuse I give myself.

My masturbatory thoughts melt away when I notice the Rubbermaid tote on the grass beside her feet.

I really hope she isn't burning what I think she's burning.

I go out the back door and notice the neighbor guy on his back porch, leering at Alice. He's conveniently outside on every rare occasion Alice is. I wonder if he thinks his creeping isn't obvious. Maybe it's not even creeping. Maybe it's just the hillbilly stare I've encountered in every redneck southwestern Ohio neighborhood I've lived in. Although, the way Alice is dressed today could probably provide him with enough mental porn for a week or more.

I quickly stride up to Alice.

She glances distractedly at me.

"What are you doing?" I ask.

"Burning this shit." She puffs on her cigarette and squints at the grill as she pushes the contents around with a stick.

"That's all my writing stuff! It's nearly twenty years' worth."

She shrugs. "You said you were going to burn it anyway."

"*I* was going to burn it. Me. It was going to be symbolic."

"Whatever. I needed the tote."

"What for?"

"Stuff."

"What stuff?"

"*My* stuff. Maybe if someone had rented a bigger house, space wouldn't be at such a premium."

I look down at the tote. It's completely empty. I hate the word 'tote'.

"I can't believe this. You didn't even think to ask me first?"

"You would have just said no. You're like a hoarder or something. You've been talking about burning this shit since we met."

"Well, it looks like you got it all. Maybe you should go inside before you give Mapes a coronary."

She glances over her shoulder at the neighbor, whose eyes are undoubtedly glued to Alice's firm little ass.

"Hi, Mr. Mapes!" she smiles and waves.

"Hey, lil girl," he drawls in his Appalachian twang.

A shudder runs through me.

I think about throwing my arms heavenward and shouting "How did I end up here!" but don't want to be that dramatic.

"Betcha feel like crying, huh?" Alice takes the last drag from her cigarette and flicks it out into the yard. I look at the grill as if to say, "Couldn't have just tossed it there?"

"No. You're right. Someone had to do it." I blink against the smoke and wipe at my eyes. "I feel more unburdened now. Like I can move on. Start the next phase of my life. Maybe take that programming class."

"You're full of shit."

FOR DINNER, we have store brand ravioli from a can, store brand potato chips, and tap water, which is probably toxic. Alice looks like she's about to cry while we eat. She's told me on more than one occasion the only thing she likes about eating is the cigarette she has afterward. I don't know if this because of the bad food we eat or if she resents the fact that eating could make you gain weight and I've never cared enough to ask.

"So," I say, "did you read any of the shit you burned?"

She flinches and pokes at a gelatinous glob of ravioli.

"Some of it." Now she looks mad. "But, you know, I can only read so much about Callie. It's boring."

"Ah-ha. That's why you burned it."

"Why did you even want to keep it around? So you could jerk off to it after I went to bed? You told me you were over her. I helped you take the last step, I guess."

"That's ridiculous. You know it's fiction, right?"

Nothing clicks in her eyes and I decide to elaborate despite the risk of sounding condescending.

"That means it's not true."

She scoffs as though offended. "I know what fiction means. I'm not that fucking stupid. Besides, if there was fucking in it at all, I know it has to be fiction. And just because you changed her name to Carly doesn't make it fiction."

I don't let her finish dinner. I stand up and grab her by the arm, dragging her into the bedroom.

She doesn't protest.

Afterward, we lie in bed, naked, feeling the cool breeze from the ceiling fan and sharing a cigarette. The window is open and Mapes's little dogs are yapping like crazy. The sound of the dogs sends me into a rage spiral and I take a drag of the cigarette and tell myself that Mapes is just a lonely, simple old guy and not a creepy 400-pound tumor who has been pressed up against his fence listening to us fuck.

"Are you going to write about me one day?" Alice asks.

"I don't think I'm going to write anymore. Besides, if I do, all of my male characters will be impotent and alone."

"Depressing."

"Viva misanthropy."

4
Dr. Jolly

DR. JOLLY IS not really a doctor. He has a framed certificate hanging on the wall of his 'office' from something called Dr. Blast's School of Enlightened Well-Being. Curious, I researched this one day and, from what I could figure out, discovered that Dr. Blast's School of Enlightened Well-Being was a mail scam that reached its heyday in the mid-seventies.

Really, he's just Claude Jolly, a rangy man with a thin white ponytail and big white beard. Dr. Jolly's Godwater was born from his love of hydration, enthusiasm for glassmaking, and good fortune.

The love of hydration stems from his boxing days, something he made a genuine go at in his late teens and early twenties (a really long time ago!). Hydration is essential for any athlete and Dr. Jolly decided he trained and fought better when his water bottle was loaded with the good old stuff from the family farm's well. Perhaps this was just an excuse for getting his ass handed to him when he ventured away from the rings of the Midwest and into more legitimate areas like New York or Las Vegas. Boxing is not something he abandoned altogether and it is not unusual to arrive at work and find him or one of his employees laid out in the parking lot. He says it's essential for the destruction of ego.

His enthusiasm for glassmaking was discovered when he retired from the ring at age twenty-four and began smoking marijuana and dropping acid to deal with the physical and emotional traumas suffered during his boxing days. He took a glassblowing class and an apprenticeship with a man who had a shop at one of the local renaissance festivals who he found wandering the grounds of his family's estate one fall morning in a mushroom-induced vision quest. He began traveling the circuit of renaissance festivals all over the US and Canada and, when there wasn't one of those to be found, he sold his wares out of his Volkswagen Vanagon in the parking lot at Grateful Dead shows. On his trips home, he would fill up his empty vessels with water from the family's well, to give them weight as much as anything. "After all," he would say, "a bottle filled with water is a bottle filled with life. An empty bottle is just an empty bottle." The philosophy behind this was inarguable.

His good fortune came when both of his parents were killed by their prized bull, Clancy. His parents had amassed a small fortune by operating a dairy farm on the outskirts of Twin Springs and that fortune landed squarely in Dr. Jolly's lap. He took the death as a sign, sold all of the cattle, closed the ice cream stand (which disappointed many of the townsfolk, as it had really become more of a low-grade amusement park and was a local staple and something of a tourist attraction), and became vegan long before it was the trendy thing to do. He sold off two-thirds of the farm to a local developer who specialized in eco-friendly housing developments long before *that* was the trendy thing to do, the amount made from this sale ensuring him he would never again need to do anything he didn't want to, as if he ever really had. He started Dr. Jolly's Godwater in the early eighties—locally sourced water in a hand-blown glass bottle with his patented E-Z Cork stopper plugged into the opening. Since his first week of operation, the demand has always been higher than the supply.

I learned none of this history from actual conversation with Dr. Jolly. It's a heavily abridged version of what can be found on his website, which runs in excess of 20,000 words. I remember applying for the job with Gus, both of us laughing about it and thinking, "Well, this won't last very long."

That was ten years ago.

I pull into Dr. Jolly's Godwater Campus (so says the ornate wrought iron sign over the long gravel driveway). The campus features a large Quonset hut where bottles are made and the water is poured, the Well of Purity, Dr. Jolly's 'office', and, farther back up a small hill, the sagging remains of the Jolly farmhouse. Dr. Jolly's office is a large tent set up beside the much larger Quonset building. He says he's sensitive to noise and prefers not to be around the sounds of industry all day. We all know he mostly stays out there, reads obscure philosophy books, and partakes of endless bottles of two-thirds Dr. Jolly's Godwater and one-third vodka, the good stuff.

He does venture into the building two or three times a day and today I find him on his hands and knees in my station, rooting around on the floor.

"Morning," I say.

He's holding something between his thumb and forefinger and muttering, "Blueberry." He picks up something else and says, "Flax seed." These are presumably from the last batch of trail mix I ate at my station, something we're not supposed to do. Or it could just be residual detritus from my beard, carried to my station from the break room.

"It's like a forest down there, huh?" I say because it doesn't really matter what you say to Dr. Jolly. He doesn't really listen to anyone.

"Place is filthy," he says. "Get a broom and sweep up before you start."

I'm convinced he still doesn't know my name.

"Sure thing," I say.

I'll probably wait until Gus comes in and tell him Dr. Jolly told me to tell him to do it.

I think about asking him for a raise, something I've been trying to work up the courage to do for the past several years, but he's out the door too quickly.

I look at the wall of twenty-ounce bottles ready to be filled, the basket of corks that will need to be twisted into them. I sit down in my chair, wheel myself up to the charged quartz faucet, and get to work.

Dr. Jolly's Godwater. Now with even MORE beard hair!

5
Charle

"HARDER?"

Smack!

The sounds of Alice come through the bedroom as my phone vibrates in my pocket and I pull it out to see my ex-wife's number on the screen. Instant panic. My body immediately erupts into a fury and I use my right hand to vigorously scratch my shin while pressing ACCEPT with my left thumb.

"Hello. Everything okay?"

Smack! Smack! Smack!

I get up from the couch and move into the kitchen.

"Everything is not okay," Jen says. "We need to talk about Charle."

Jen usually skips any pleasantries and gets right to the point. Charle is my fifteen-year-old son. We named him Charle after much debate. I wanted to name him Charles, after the only grandfather I liked, thought maybe we could call him Chuck—a robust, manly sounding name—but Jen had said Charles sounded "too plural." So I'd sarcastically suggested Charle and that's what stuck. We should have known the boy would be fucked up since he started life as a passive aggressive argument.

"What's up?"

"He bit another kid's finger off at the Academy."

"Well . . . did the other kid deserve it? Wait . . . another?"

"That's not the point."

"Do you need me to talk to him?"

She laughs. "Um, no, definitely not. His therapists and I have decided you're part of the problem."

"So what can I do to help?" I know what she's about to ask. When we got divorced, she moved to Florida to be closer to her parents, thus putting me, physically, out of the picture.

"I need you to start sending me a couple hundred dollars a month so we can move him to a better school."

The Academy is basically a military school and, I imagine, not very cheap.

"I'm already paying child support. And I'm barely scraping by as it is. I don't think there's any way I can do that."

"Are you serious?"

"Um, yeah, pretty serious. I'm living off water and party pizzas. I think my insides are rotting. I have a rash."

"Haven't you had the same job for like ten years? Can't your teenage slut pay some of the bills?"

This is why I had to get off MyFace. I'm not a paranoid person but Jen has proven time and time again that she stalks my movements and if there is ever a public demonstration of me remotely enjoying life, she will do whatever she can to put a stop to it. We don't have any mutual friends and don't talk much, so that's the only way she can know about these things.

"Okay," I say. "First of all, Alice isn't a teenager." I think about saying, "And she's not a slut," but, I don't know, maybe she is. I'm just not judgmental about it. Instead I say, "And asking her to pay for our son's transgressions is a little fucked up."

"'Transgressions?' What kind of a word is that? Oh, and speaking of words, when are you gonna get that big book sale? I mean, that's what you like to do, right? Write stupid little books? You sure didn't have time for me when we were together. Isn't that why you've never gotten a real job."

"I don't really do that much anymore."

"Oh, so your little teen slut's good enough to give it up for but the mother of your only child wasn't."

Ultimately, this is what the phone call is about. It's not really about the money to send Charle to a better school. It's more about her making me feel small, like a deadbeat loser. It's something I think of as a semi-annual adjustment to my ego.

"Look, I'm not going to be able to send you an additional two hundred bucks a month, but I'll see what I can do."

"What about your tax return? Don't you have anything left from that?"

"Tax return?" I laugh. "I never paid off my student loans. They take that every year. They have ever since I dropped out."

She scoffs.

Alice wanders into the kitchen. She's naked, red stripes streaking her tiny pale ass.

"Thanks for wasting my time," Jen says.

"Um, you called me."

"Do you know how useless you are?"

"Thank god if I ever forget, I have you there to remind me."

"Send me what you can. It's important. *Charle* is important."

Charle is important. Almost like an afterthought.

"Yeah. I'll see what I can do. Tell him I love him, okay?"

She chuffs out a laugh, says, "Yeah, okay," and hangs up.

"Who was that?" Alice says, even though I'm pretty sure she knows.

"That was my conscience."

6
Easy J's Travel Plaza

SOME GUYS HANG out at bars or around TVs watching sports or playing video games. Gus and I like to hang out at Easy J's Travel Plaza, a truck stop off I-675. It's something of a Friday ritual. We'd also done it when neither one of us felt like going to work, opting to spend a day in the Easy J Inn, their restaurant, watching the various truckers and other patrons come and go. The people watching is what sets Easy J's apart from bars. Hip bars are full of trendy, reasonably attractive people ostensibly on their way up. Dive bars are great but are often too crowded on Friday nights and they're filled with gruff people who have nothing to lose. Fuel these people with cheap, additive-laden booze, and it gets a bit scary. Many of them are often of a certain redneck, blue-collar persuasion, and Gus and I stick out like sore thumbs. We tried it exactly once but our long hair and beards were like calling cards for abuse. We debated trying a biker look but ultimately decided there was something overwhelmingly soft about us we would not be able to cover up with any amount of leather or patches. Jerry Garcia could not become Lemmy from Motorhead overnight.

"I'm ready to try it again," Gus says.

"Try what?"

"Infiltrating the well."

I've already put our previous botched attempt out of my head.

"Remind me again why you want to do this?" I ask.

"Principles. Symbolism. Metaphor."

"What if people end up getting sick?"

"Then it won't really be a well of purity, will it? Plus . . . think about it . . . Doesn't Dr. Jolly drive you insane? The way he walks around all high and mighty and self-righteous . . . for doing absolutely nothing at all! He hires people to make bottles. He hires people to fill them. He hires people to drive them to stores. While he sits in his stupid tent office and drinks and reads and listens to weirdo music."

"I like weirdo music."

"That's not the point. Shouldn't he be grateful? I mean, come on, the dude hasn't had to work since he was like in his thirties. We make his life easy. What does he even need money for? He doesn't have any kids. He's not expanding or franchising or anything. He doesn't donate any of it that I know of. He just hoards it. Meanwhile, people like you and me are fucking struggling. I mean, I'm paying for you to eat tonight at a shitty greasy spoon truck stop because you can't afford it."

"I can afford it. You offered."

"That's not the point. Maybe you can barely afford it, but you would still feel the cost of it. Like, you would have to ask yourself, 'Can I afford ten dollars to eat with Gus tonight?' I know I had to ask myself that. And we shouldn't have to! We work full-time fucking jobs. If we want to have a night out to eat or drink a couple beers or watch a fucking movie, we should be able to do it without thinking about it, without feeling guilty about it. I still live with my fucking mom!"

"How is infiltrating the well going to change any of that?"

"Because we'll know."

"Know what?"

"That Dr. Jolly is a fake."

"And how does that help us?"

"Self-satisfaction."

"It seems like it would almost make it worse. Like, it's bad enough that we're essentially helping Dr. Jolly live whatever life he wants to live. Wouldn't it be worse if we were also helping him sell water from a well of purity, filtered through a charged crystal faucet, even if it were garbage water? It just seems like then we'd knowingly be aiding him in the perpetuation of a lie. Like if we just went into our job and filled fancy bottles with municipal tap water. At least this way we can convince ourselves he's maybe sort of special because he inherited rights to some kind of sacred water reservoir."

Gus shakes his head. "Do you really believe that?"

"Not really. But sometimes I want to."

"Anyway, like I said before, it's about principles."

"Is this about not getting a raise?"

"That certainly plays into it."

"Have you ever asked him for one?"

"No. Have you?"

"No."

"Fuck. That's why he employs people like us. The spineless. The weak. The failures. We'll never be fired, but we'll never get a raise either. Because we fuck up too much. Like, it's hard to ask for a raise when you call in or just don't show up three-to-eight times a month."

"I've considered that. Why do we fuck up so much?"

"It's in our blood. We were born to be stout working class Appalachians. We were not meant to eat the fruit from the tree of knowledge. The second we picked up our first book and developed big ideas, we disqualified ourselves. Maybe college would have helped but we have enough wild hillbilly in us to feel imprisoned by it. We should be mountain philosophers, drunk or stoned all the time, holding venomous snakes in one hand and filling notebooks with the other. We should have insects and rodents in our beards."

At the thought of insects living in my beard, I scratch my inner wrist.

"Have I told you about my rash?" I say.

"You have a rash?"

"Yeah. It's spreading all over."

I hold my arm across the table and lift up my sleeve. Even though it's summer, I've been wearing thin long sleeve shirts to cover the unsightly blemishes and lesions. I fit in nicely with the heroin addicts in my neighborhood.

He moves his head closer to my arm.

"What is it?" he says.

"I don't know. It's a rash."

"What's causing it?"

"If I knew that, I wouldn't have it."

"It's probably bed bugs. Have you tried researching it?"

"I'm afraid to."

"Are you going to the doctor?"

"I don't really have the money."

"We have insurance."

"I don't even know if I have money for the copay but I guess I'll have to if it keeps getting worse. It's driving me insane."

"Maybe it's stress."

"Could be. If that's the case, I think I'm stuck with it."

"Don't worry. Once we infiltrate the well you'll feel a lot better."

7
Infiltration Take Two

"YOU GOTTA SEE THIS," Gus says.

He unties the strap holding the door to the bed of his truck closed. It's dark on the narrow gravel road out behind the Well of Purity and it takes my eyes a second to focus on what he has reached back and slid out to rest on the door. It looks like a bag of shit tied to a cinderblock and smells terrible.

"What is it?"

"It's a bag of shit tied to a cinderblock."

"And . . .?" But I don't really need to ask. I know what its purpose is.

"Don't be a pussy, okay? We're not going to make anyone sick. Think about it . . . there's nothing covering the well. Do you know how many birds have shit in it? Shat in it. Whatever. How many dying insects and amphibians are in it? How many animals have probably fallen into it to rot? For all we know, it's the contaminants that keep people coming back. It's why it's so damn popular. It's like a tea made from rot and decay."

"It's popular because it's the only local artisanal water around and

31

everyone living in Twin Springs can afford it. Have you ever drank it?"

"No. You?"

"Can't afford it."

Gus struggles to pick up the shitterblock.

"I'm not helping you with that," I say.

"I should be able to manage it."

We have to stop twice so Gus can rest and smoke a cigarette before we reach the Well of Purity. We had once decided to acronymize Well of Purity but, seeing as we got 'WOP', we decided it was too racially insensitive to be a keeper so the most we ever shortened it to was 'the well.'

Even though we're both pretty sure Jolly is long passed out, we glance up at the sagging farmhouse before hopping the rusted tensile fence surrounding the well. The only light is the porchlight. We close the distance between the fence and the well. Gus exhaustedly sets the shitterblock on the low rock wall surrounding the well. He lights another cigarette.

"Can I get one of those?" I ask. "Ceremony."

He hands me the pack and I pull one out and light it up.

Gus is still catching his breath in between draws and is less chatty than usual. I take deep drags and exhale the smoke, smelling the scent of damp grass and earth and hay mixing with it, looking up at all the stars in the clear sky. Ohio's all right in the summer, I think. But that's about it. And that's only really in the rural areas. Where I live in Dayton, summer is just a cesspool of motorcycles and feral children and heated up dog shit and the barking of the dogs releasing that shit and morbidly obese people wearing not enough clothes.

Gus flicks his cigarette butt toward the well and it goes flying out in the opposite direction.

He bends down to grab onto the shitterblock and says, "This has to work."

He lifts the cinderblock and, from down in the well, we hear: "Who's there?"

A startled expression sprains Gus's face and he quickly drops the shitterblock.

We both take off running toward the truck.

After only a few steps, Gus collapses to the ground and at first I think he's tripped over a knot of grass or maybe even just his own feet.

I contemplate running but whatever remaining conscience I have stops me and I turn around to go check on Gus.

He's not doing well.

He's out cold, his head dented and bloody.

The shitterblock lies a few feet behind him.

I don't know what to do.

I try to think if a falling cinderblock is enough to kill a person. It seems possible but I don't really know physics or whatever. I contemplate bending to check his pulse but think it would probably be a bad idea to leave my fingerprints on him. I think about calling 911 but I'm trespassing and don't think that will look that great. Plus, Dr. Jolly was presumably in the well and could be coming up on us at any minute.

I should just run but I feel paralyzed.

Then I see him coming through the darkness, naked and pale.

"Halt!" he says.

I'm caught.

This is not good.

"Who's there?" he says.

I take a couple of steps toward him, my arms up.

"It's me, sir."

He squints as I move closer to him.

"Why are you raising your arms?"

"I don't know. Because I got caught."

He's now standing above Gus's prone body.

"This seems to be the bigger problem," he says.

I put my arms down and move across from him to stare down at Gus's body.

"What were you two doing?"

FAILURE AS A WAY OF LIFE

We are clearly trespassing. My best friend is currently lying facedown in the grass, his head bashed in with a cinderblock. To tell Dr. Jolly we were there to throw a cinderblock with a bag of shit tied to it into the Well of Purity—his pride, his life's work, his reason for existence—seems overwhelmingly bleak.

"Sometimes we just like to look at it?"

"What? The well?"

"Yes, sir."

He has spotted the shitterblock.

"It looks like you were trying to drop that into the well."

"Um . . . that was Gus's idea." I figure if Gus is dead, it doesn't really matter, right? The accomplice always gets off lighter than the perpetrator.

"It looks like you were trying to drop that bag of whatever into the well. And since it seems to be tied to a cinderblock, I have reason to believe you've tried it before to no avail. Am I correct?"

I clear my throat and say, "You're not not correct."

Dr. Jolly nudges Gus with his foot. "He's been a faithful employee, hasn't he?"

I guess. If you don't consider habitually trying to throw shit (literally and figuratively) into the well.

"Yes, sir. One of the best," I say.

"Let's get him over to the well."

"Shouldn't we . . . call someone?"

"This will be a lot less messy."

Gus is a fairly big guy and I'm pretty weak so I let Dr. Jolly do most of the heavy lifting, trying my hardest not to look at his cock and saggy old man sack swinging like a fleshy, hairy pendulum between his legs.

We get him over to the well. Dr. Jolly, who's taken hold of his shoulders, is covered in blood.

"Can we set him down for a second?" I say.

"You'll have to put him down anyway. I'm the only one who can throw him in the well."

"We're going to . . .?"

"Of course. What did you think we were going to do with him?"

We set Gus in the grass beside the well. I bend down and fish his wallet, phone, and keys from his pockets.

"That all you need?" Jolly says.

I nod solemnly.

"Okay." He bends down and grabs Gus under the arms. "Heave ho." He lifts him up and flips him over the wall of the well.

I hear a splash.

"Do you have any more business here?" Jolly asks.

"No, sir."

"Then maybe you should go. See you Monday."

I walk back to the truck. I'll drive it to Gus's apartment complex and call Alice to come and pick me up. I probably won't tell her what happened.

I then imagine me sitting in Gus's truck in front of his mom's house while repeatedly texting Alice with no response and then decide, fuck it, I'll just drive his truck back to my house. I'm shaken and it's hard to think.

When I get home Alice is already in bed. I find it slightly peculiar she works mostly during the day since hiring a cam girl seems to me like it would be mostly an impulsive, drunken late night endeavor. I lie on the couch and stare at the ceiling, hearing the sound of Gus hitting the water and digging at my irritated skin. I think it's unlikely I'm ever going to fall asleep but have apparently underestimated my exhaustion and my capacity for apathy because the next thing I know I wake to the sound of Alice in the kitchen making coffee.

I'm momentarily confused but the previous night comes back to me all at once, the various eruptions about my body lighting up and screaming. It usually gets worse later in the day and the fact it's already started seems exceptionally foreboding.

I pull my phone out of my pocket, half-expecting to find a message from Gus.

But of course there can't be. I have his phone.

I get off the couch and move into the kitchen, scratching myself.

"Are you making breakfast?" I ask.

"Yeah. Toast and eggs. Coffee."

I only eat breakfast on the weekends. This is what we have every Saturday and Sunday morning.

"Sounds great," I say.

"I need to take the car today," she says.

"Okay. I have Gus's truck if I need to go anywhere."

"Why do you have Gus's truck?"

"Um . . . I had to drive him home last night."

"You guys go out?"

"Sort of."

"Sounds fun. I was stuck here all night."

"You had the car. You could have gone anywhere."

"With who?"

It's true. Alice doesn't have any friends. I should have probably seen that as some kind of sign.

"You're right. I should have asked if you wanted to come." I decide to go ahead and say it before she can. If she said it first then I would feel immediately defensive and it would inevitably lead to an argument.

"It's okay. I had a couple of long sessions. Made a few bucks. Pussy's kind of sore and I might have damaged my asshole."

"Speaking of which," I say. "Do you think there's any way you could give me a little extra this month?"

By this I mean a little extra than the nothing she's given me since moving in.

"I don't know," she says. "You know most of what I make goes right back into it." By this she means the money she makes is mostly spent buying make-up, underwear, and clothes "to keep things new."

"Whatever," I shrug. "It's just been a little tight. That's all."

"Maybe we need a roommate or something."

I wonder how bad my rash would get if I had to go to work knowing

Alice was home alone with someone else.

"That'd be a last resort," I say before tucking into my eggs and toast.

8
An Anxious Weekend

IT'S AN ANXIETY-FILLED weekend. I do my best not to think about what happened to Gus but it's always somewhere in the forefront of my thoughts, along with all the other things I typically worry about.

Alice takes the car out Saturday afternoon and returns in the early evening with a slight limp. I think about asking her about it, decide I don't want to hear whatever weird lie she will tell me, and go out to mow the grass.

A thin older man with slicked back white hair reaching down to his shoulders watches me the entire time while smoking cigarettes and ashing them into what looks like an ashtray intended for a car he holds cupped in his left hand. He wears a racing t-shirt tucked into stone-washed jeans and is clearly white trash, as is everyone in my neighborhood, but conducts himself with an almost dapper elegance.

I finish and shut off the lawnmower.

"Excellent form, my friend," he says.

The sweat and the sun have set the rash on fire and I'm scratching my damp arms vigorously.

"Uh, thanks," I say.

He crushes his cigarette out in the car ashtray and takes a step toward me.

"I'm the Monarch," he says.

It seems like a completely fitting name. I imagine him drifting around the neighborhood all day, the gracefulness of a butterfly, the haughty air of royalty.

If I had a nickname, what would it be? The Cuckold? The Asshole? The Used? The Discarded? The Worthless? The Bum? The Rash? The Anxious? The Depressed? The Misanthrope? The Poor? The Doomed? The Ill-Fated? The Neglectful? The Powerless? The Lazy? The Slump-Shouldered?

Instead I just say, "I'm Ryan," and hold out my sweaty hand, who knows how much dead skin and blood under the fingernails, assuming he will find some reason not to take it.

He takes it anyway. It's a perfectly royal handshake.

"I live there at the end of the street. You need anything, don't hesitate to stop by."

"Thanks, man," I say.

He glances at the lawnmower. "You don't suppose I could borrow that for a couple hours, do you?"

This man has just offered me anything–anything. How could I say no? Even if I'm pretty sure he lives in a house as small as mine and that house is probably filled with a hoard of broken, shitty things of absolutely no value to anyone. But that's just me being judgmental and condescending.

"Sure," I say. "Need me to gas it up for you?"

"Nah. I got gas. I'll send someone for it."

He pulls his pack of off-brand cigarettes from his pocket and lights one up. I notice they're 100s and stop myself from asking for one.

"Nice day," he says. "Nice day." Then he turns and walks back up the street.

Mapes is open-mouthed and drooling in his front yard, his three dogs yapping and straining at their leashes.

The Monarch nods toward him and says, "Howdy do?"

Mapes must be really medicated today because he doesn't say anything. Just looks down and focuses in real tight on one of his dogs' assholes.

I go into the house and take a shower. It's the first one I've had in a couple of weeks and I only take it because I think it might help with the rash. I make a dinner of tomato soup and Cheez-it for Alice and me and spend the rest of the evening sitting in my chair in the living room, scratching my rash and wondering what I'm going to do. The shower did not help with the rash. It's almost like it just shined the rash up, making it glow in fierce red streaks.

The next day a boy who looks about twelve knocks on the door and tells me he's returning the lawnmower. I go out and put the lawnmower in the garage, notice the Monarch talking to Mapes on his front porch. I don't want to get embroiled in a conversation or anything so I slip back into the house without waving or saying hi.

I wait until it sounds like Alice is finished with a session and knock on the bedroom door to see what she wants for lunch.

She's lying on the bed, her laptop open beside her, smoking a cigarette.

I notice the Rubbermaid tote I'd used to store my manuscripts in sitting beside the bed, the top removed.

I can't help looking inside it.

It's full of dildos.

"You burned my manuscripts so you could have storage for dildos?" I try not to sound mad or heartbroken.

"Where else was I gonna put them? It's not like I can just leave them laying around."

"It's not exactly like we ever have company."

"Would you want to look at bottles of water all the time when you came home?"

She has a point. "I guess you're right. What do you want for lunch?"

"I'm skipping it. I'm getting fat."

I glance up and down her naked, lightly tattooed body. She is definitely not fat.

"You're not fat," I say. "You need to eat."

"I'll eat dinner."

It's pointless to argue with her.

I go into the kitchen and open a can of tuna—the cheap stuff—and eat it directly from the can. Then I wonder if maybe my rash is caused by mercury or something. After eating, I go into the living room and sit in my chair and mindlessly watch MeTube videos. Nothing specific. Mostly just normal people talking about stuff and it just makes me remember my one real friend might be dead.

That night I receive another call from the unknown number.

Again the caller says nothing.

I imagine the caller again as a female, quiet, dark-haired, maybe only a few years younger than me, very pale. Wherever she is, it's earlier than it is here and today it's clear, the early evening sunlight filtering through thin curtains and filling whatever room she's sitting in. After thinking about it, I realize it's like a dream room that serves no purpose. There's nothing in it except the chair she's sitting in, as though the room only exists for her to call strangers.

9
Gus 2.0

I take Gus's truck to work on Monday morning and am greeted with the sight of the upper half of his ass staring at me when I turn into the filling room. I've never been so happy to see his ass before.

"Gus!" I say.

"Oh, hey man." He throws his hand up and finishes filling the bottle he's working on before turning in his chair to face me. "You got my truck and my phone and shit?"

"Yeah. I drove it to work today."

I take his phone out of my pocket and hand it to him. I don't really know why I brought it in with me. I don't like to be responsible for things. My intention was to probably leave it on his desk.

He turns his phone on and quickly scrolls through it.

I move closer to him, inspecting him while his attention is elsewhere.

He radiates something he's never radiated before. He practically glows. There is a scent coming from him that isn't as displeasing as the patchouli he typically uses to cover up intense BO and what I'd always assumed was improper or just lazy ass wiping. It was never the patchouli I found displeasing.

I inspect his head. There doesn't seem to be a mark on it.

"I thought . . ." I trail off, not really knowing what I thought. That he was dead, I guess. Or at least very badly injured or perhaps even drowned. I'm so overwhelmed with relief I have to sit down.

He glances up. "Yeah. Want to go to lunch?"

I don't have any money. "I guess I can get coffee or something," I say.

"Don't worry, man. I'll get it." Then he mouths, "I got a raise."

And, like that, all of my relief and goodwill is replaced with a seething rage. Not at Gus. At this point, it's hard to see Gus as anything but some kind of risen messiah. The rage is at Dr. Jolly.

So I guess that's how it goes. He has to practically kill you before he'll give you a raise. The raise is probably just hush money to make sure Gus doesn't blab to anyone about how Dr. Jolly threw him in the well so he wouldn't be responsible for someone getting killed on his property. I think about throwing myself behind Dr. Jolly's car except that, now that I think about it, I've never seen him drive and don't even know if he owns a car. I think about accidentally breaking one of the bottles as I'm filling it, brutally slashing my wrists, but that seems too much like the suicide I meditate on every three months or so.

"Okay. Cool," I say. "Around noon?"

"Sounds good."

I plug my earbuds into my phone, cue up some music, and get to work. I find that if you don't have something to drown out the sound of water constantly running, all you have to do is piss all day.

AT LUNCH, we drive into Twin Springs and I get a sandwich and coffee from Pete's Market, the grocery store. Gus buys a pack of cigarettes on our way out. We find a park bench in front of an herb garden and sit down. It's warm, the sunlight making my rash itch. I fight the urge to scratch.

"So . . .?" I unwrap my sandwich.

"I know. Friday was weird, huh?"

"To say the least. I thought you were dead or something."

"I probably would have been if it hadn't been for the bag of shit."

"The bag of shit?" I'd already forgotten about it.

"Yeah. It must have softened the blow or something. The impact was still enough to knock me out."

"But there was blood."

"There was shit," he said. "Maybe you thought it was blood, but it was definitely shit. Like diarrhea shit. I gotta start eating better."

"Kinda surprised you didn't drown."

"Oh, yeah, that. I think the water revived me. And, I don't know, Jolly must be down there a lot because there's like a permanent ladder on the side. I panicked for a couple of minutes until I put things together and found it and climbed up. It's probably why he seems so fit and wiry. That's hard fucking work. I climbed up and didn't have my phone so I walked out to the road and saw that my truck was gone so I just went to the hut and waited for Jolly. He let me in and I just started working. Didn't know what else to do."

"You didn't think about calling me to pick you up or anything?"

"Nah. Honestly, I felt a little dazed. Kinda weird. Sorta stoned almost."

"And you've been in there working since Friday night?"

He laughs. "It does sound kind of crazy, doesn't it?"

"And you got a raise?"

"Yeah. That happened Sunday morning. I think Jolly felt kind of guilty or something."

"How much?"

"I'm not allowed to discuss it."

"Come on."

"I promised. Let's just say my money problems are over. I don't spend much money anyway but now I might even be able to start saving something."

What he describes sounds like an enviable position. I'd blown off college and opted for slacker jobs right out of high school, blaming my then marriage and spending most of my free time on writing, telling myself if it was ever going to pay off, it might be big. Over the years I'd seen the publishing industry slowly decay, became a lot less naive about who actually gets published by large publishers, and a lot more aware of the fact I was writing shit no one really wanted to read. Still, I never opted to find a better job, telling myself if I just stayed at Jolly's and kept quiet and worked hard, I might be able to eke out some kind of living. Which I guess I was doing but it was so tied up in deprivation I didn't know if I could really describe it as living.

"That . . . sounds great," I say.

"I feel rejuvenated," he says. "I think maybe there *is* something to Dr. Jolly's Godwater. I think I'm going to start bathing in it . . . Now that I can afford to. But maybe only like once a week."

I take a bite of my sandwich and furiously scratch my forearm.

We finish our sandwiches and sit on the bench and smoke cigarettes. A girl walks by on the sidewalk in front of us and I notice Gus's leering gaze fall upon her. She's wearing black stretch pants and a tie-dyed t-shirt. She has a bandana tied do-rag style over her head. She smiles and then stops.

"Hey there," she says to Gus.

"Hey," he says and I wonder if they know each other.

"Could I possibly bum a smoke?" she says, acting somewhat embarrassed.

Gus pulls the pack from his shirt pocket and says, "Hey, wait, are you even eighteen?"

She smiles again and says, "About a decade ago."

"Okay," Gus says. He pulls a cigarette out and hands it to her, lights it for her.

I expect her to walk on but she says, "Scooch over," and sits next to Gus.

They begin talking and I faze out for a couple of minutes. When my cigarette's finished, I crush it out and stand to toss it in the trashcan by the street.

"We should probably get back," I say, interrupting them.

Gus pulls his phone out and checks the time. "Yeah, I guess we should," he says. Then, to the girl, he says, "Are you on MyFace?"

"Of course," she says.

"What's your name?"

"I'm on there under Leslie Feldmeyer, but everyone calls me Tarot."

Gus is looking at his phone. "Found you. Sent you a friend request."

"Oh, cool," she says. "I don't have my phone on me. I'll accept it when I get home. Thanks for the smoke."

"Want one for the road?"

"Sure," she says and Gus hands her another one.

We get in the truck and I say, "You've got it."

"What?" he says.

"I don't know. It. Whatever *it* is."

We drive the short drive to work, out in the countryside, and I wonder if I can handle my best friend being successful.

10
Fucking Republicans

I PULL INTO the driveway, the dread I feel as soon as I get off the highway and enter Dayton now fully settled in my core. There's a fancy Cadillac parked on the curb in front of the house and my first thought is that it's the landlord and we've done something wrong. Maybe it's illegal to do sex work in the house. I don't know.

I give myself a thorough scratchdown before getting out of the car. I've tried to keep the scratching to a minimum around Alice. She hasn't mentioned the quite visible rash as of yet. It's probably because she keeps her eyes closed on the rare occasions we actually have sex and she never touches any part of me except my cock. Otherwise I think she tries not to look at me so she can pretend she's living with someone else. I can't really blame her.

A fat, sweaty man, probably in his fifties, exits the house and begins walking toward his Cadillac. He's smiling broadly and gives me a wave.

"Hoo boy!" he says.

The front door's unlocked and I go into the house to find Alice naked and smoking a cigarette in bed.

"Did you . . .?" I begin.

"I was waiting for you," she says.

47

I waste no time in stripping off my clothes and getting into bed with her even though I feel really bad about myself. She goes down on me for the first time in I don't know how long but the only thing I can really think about is the guy leaving the house. I wouldn't doubt it if Alice were fucking guys on the side and I wonder if it bothers me more that the guy seemed like a rich, old, fat Republican. Like it implies Alice has no standards. Which goes a long way toward explaining why she's with me but also makes me feel even worse about myself. Has she transitioned from a cam girl into a prostitute? If so, I again feel as though this is my fault. Because of my low income and lack of drive, the arguably most attractive and inarguably youngest girlfriend I've ever had is now forced to fuck Republicans for money.

I'm not getting hard.

"What's wrong?" she says.

"I don't know," I say, even though I'm pretty sure I do know what's wrong and it's the thought of another man having his cock inside of her a very short while ago.

She tries bringing me to life with her hand.

"Who was that guy I saw leaving?"

"The cable guy."

"We don't have cable."

"I was thinking about getting it."

"Cable guys drive Cadillacs?"

She rolls her eyes and takes her hand off me.

"The sales people do. You really want to talk about this now?"

"Is there a better time?"

"Okay, you got me. He's a client, okay?"

"Jesus. Did you fuck him?"

She frowns. "Is that what you think I do all day? Whore around? Fuck you. He just wanted to spank me for a little while. It's all pretty harmless. See?"

She gets up on her knees and turns around so I can see the big red handprints on her ass.

I'm suddenly hard.

I get up on my knees and move behind her.

"Don't care so much now, huh?" she says.

When finished, we lie on the sweat-dampened sheet under the ceiling fan.

"I think I hate Gus," I say.

"Who's Gus?" she says and I wonder if she's ever listened to a word I've said.

11
No Returns

PAY UP!

The words are scrawled in dripping red spraypaint across the windshield of my car. The driver's side window is smashed out, the rock that presumably did the deed sitting in the driver's seat. Anger surges through me but ultimately I just feel like crying. I stand looking at my vandalized car and absently scratching my left arm.

The Monarch shuffles up next to me, virtually soundless. He's drinking beer from a can in a koozie. It's like nine o'clock in the morning.

"Guess you better pay up, huh?" he says.

"Did you see who did this?"

"Big guy in a big black truck. Didn't have time to stop him."

Bart. Jen's brother. It had to be. He's a complete and total psychopath and the fact that I'm now on his bad side is a whole other level of dread I have to deal with.

The Monarch goes over to the driver's side of the car and mimics the scene as he describes it.

"He just turned around in your driveway, pulled up right next to your car, painted that message, and threw the rock threw the window."

At this he extends the hand holding the beer toward the window before taking a big drink.

"I was thinking it probably went down like that."

"Want to come back to my place and grab a beer? You look like you could use it."

"Nah. I was on my way to work. I guess I'll have to see if my friend can take me."

"I'd let you take my car but it's got four flats right now."

"That's all right. Thanks anyway."

I go back into the house and call Gus. He tells me he wasn't planning on going to work today and asks if I want to go to Easy J's and get breakfast. I say sure.

While waiting for him I duct tape a trash bag to the driver's side door to replace the window and do my best to get the shards of glass off the seat. I wonder if I should save the rock for evidence but decide it's not really necessary. I'm not reporting this to the police so I just toss it into the woods at the end of the street. I'll have to try googling the best way to remove spraypaint from a windshield.

"Dermatitis herpetiformis," Gus says from across the booth at Easy J's.

"Whatitty whattus?" I say.

"Your rash. I think that's what it is. Probably too much gluten."

"I don't even know what that is."

"Neither do I, but it's probably in everything."

"I'm pretty sure it's just stress."

"Either way it's probably not going away anytime soon."

"Thanks for being so hopeful. Did you trim your beard?"

He shrugs. I don't know what this means. His beard is cropped close to his face. It almost looks like he has a jawline. His usually muddy brown and graying hair is pulled back into an artfully sloppy man bun and has an almost golden shine to it.

The waitress creeps up to the table. It's Maybelline, our favorite.

She's rail thin, has a lazy eye, and looks like she's had a rough life. We order our food. It's probably all loaded with gluten.

"Maybe you should go to the doctor and get it checked out," Gus says.

"I can't afford to go to the doctor. We've been over this. Plus I probably don't want to know what's wrong with me. It sounds like herpes or something, if it's what you said it was."

"I don't think gluten causes herpes. Maybe you should take a bath in the Godwater."

"I think that would be more expensive than going to the doctor."

"Do you want me to drop you off at work when we leave here?"

"Nah. I've already committed to not going. I should go but I'm just not feeling it."

"Yeah. That's the way I felt last night when I went to bed. I thought, 'I'm not going to work tomorrow.' I'm salary now anyway, so fuck it."

"You're salary?"

"Yep. I can work two hours a week or fifty. It's all the same."

"I'm not really sure—"

He waves me away as if he doesn't want to hear any rational argument.

Maybelline brings two plates of heaping food and sets them on the table. Now it's hard to see it as anything other than fuel for the rash, but I'm starving so I tear into it anyway.

About halfway through, Gus catches my eye and nods my attention over to the register.

There's a morbidly obese woman in a muumuu arguing with a different waitress behind the register.

"Your sign says 'Satisfaction Guaranteed.' I ain't satisfied," the obese woman says.

"Then why did you eat everything?"

"Cause I was hungry!"

"If you'd let us know you weren't satisfied we could have fixed it for you. But it's a little late now. Best I can do is ten percent off."

"That ain't good enough. I ain't got time to sit around and wait for you bums to try and get it right. Should get it right the first time."

"I'm terribly sorry. There's nothing we can do now."

"I want my money back."

"I can't do that."

"You know what then? You can take back your shitty food."

The woman slaps her meaty hands down on the counter, bracing herself, leans over and begins vomiting her breakfast all over the counter.

The waitress steps back quickly, a look of horror on her face.

"Ted!" she calls to the back. "Get up here!"

A man with close-cropped gray hair emerges from the back and says, "Dear Lord. Lady, you need to get out of here."

"Not until I get my refund."

The man opens the register, pulls out some cash, and drops it into the puke.

"Real nice!" the woman shouts. "Real classy!"

She delicately plucks the bills up and shakes them off before putting them in her massive purse.

She turns to leave, a look of sublime satisfaction on her face.

"Well that was exciting," I say.

"This place is great."

"Not sure I'm hungry anymore, though."

"You ready to take off?"

12
Cost of Living

I STRIP OUT of my clothes before getting in the shower. Showers have always been a somewhat rare thing for me but especially so in the last six months, for a couple of reasons. One of those reasons is the lack of sex with Alice. Another is my lack of raise at work. At the very least, I feel entitled to a cost of living raise, especially since I've been there for ten years and never received a single raise. Since I haven't received even this token bump in pay, I decided to remove most things associated with the cost of living. I have to eat, but since I can't afford to eat good food, I don't. Lately Gus has been paying for most of my meals out with his raise and I buy the cheapest shit possible when I go to the grocery store. I haven't bought new clothes in I don't know how long and only wash them when they became offensive to me. I have pretty poor hygiene standards to begin with, so this isn't very often. I haven't shaved or cut my hair in over a year. And I really only shower if intimate relations with Alice are a guaranteed thing or I do something outside that makes me sweaty or itchy. I keep waiting for Dr. Jolly to ask me about my nearly homeless appearance and smell so I can shrug and say, "Eh, cost of living, you know?" but he's never asked and probably never will. It occurs to me all of this may be contributing to the rash, but the internet has offered no help. Some sites say bathing merely throws off your skin's biome and removes the good bacteria. Other sites say bacteria is filthy and you need to wash at least periodically to avoid the plague.

The rash is horrendous. I inspect myself in the mirror. There are now a couple of patches on my face. It's on my earlobes and down both sides of my torso. All down the inside of my arms. My palms. My knees and shins. The tops of my feet. It's in the crack of my ass and, oh fuck, even on my cock. So not only is it itchy as hell, I'm turning into a fucking monster. And since it's on my cock I assume it's something sexual in nature. Probably something from Alice. Maybe this is why she's never acknowledged it.

My phone vibrates loudly on the vanity.

It's a text from Jen: "Hope you got my message."

I assume she means the rock her brother threw through my car window.

I don't think it warrants a response but know if I don't say something I'll keep thinking I should say something and this will create anxiety, which will probably make the rash worse.

"I'll send you what I have," I text. And it's not a lie. I'll send her what I have when I pay the bills at the end of the month and what I have will be exactly nothing. Just like it is every month.

"Maybe your dad could help out," she texts.

What do I say to this? I don't want him to help out. I'm already a forty-year-old man who barely feels grown up. I haven't asked my dad for money in years and really don't want to start now.

"Not an option," I text. "Maybe yours? Gotta go."

"You're a FUCKING PIECE OF SHIT!!!"

I fight the urge to throw the phone on the floor and get in the shower. I run the water hot and scrub at the rash with the washcloth, knowing my skin will feel dry later and the rash will be even worse. Maybe I need to get some lotion or something. Do I even have money to get some sort of lotion? If I had to put it practically all over my body, how long would a bottle even last? In the shower used to be one of the best times to think of story and book ideas. Now I'm incapable of thinking about anything other than the dark turn my life has taken and the even darker turns guaranteed in the future.

I step out of the shower and scrub myself dry with the towel. It's a way of scratching the rash without actually touching it. I step out of the bathroom and take a couple steps to the bedroom. I don't hear Alice in there so I open the door. She's on her back with the laptop on her stomach but doesn't seem to be working. The bedroom smells really bad.

"Why does it smell like farts in here?" I ask.

"Some guys like it," she says absently.

"Like the smell of farts?" I don't really mind the smell of my own but have never been too into smelling other people's.

"Well, I don't think they can really smell it. They like to hear girls do it."

"You're not going to say 'fart,' are you?"

"I don't like that word."

I pull a drawer out to grab some underwear.

"So . . . guys like to hear you fart? They pay for that?"

"Most guys are into a lot of weird things."

"I think if that's what they're into then they're trying too hard."

"It's not like they can help it. They're into what they're into."

I quickly put on some shorts and a t-shirt. She still hasn't mentioned the rash and I find myself dressing quickly around her.

Now that the rash has spread to my cock, I'm not sure we'll ever have sex again. Maybe that will help me clear my head. I've considered asking her to leave before but then we would end up having sex and I'd feel guilty for asking her to leave. We've been together nearly a year. I actually didn't think she was going to move with me when we found this house. It was like, once all of her stuff was packed, I thought she would realize it could just as easily be moved anywhere. Now I figure it's just a matter of time before she stockpiles enough money to get a place of her own or finds someone else who could give her a remotely decent life. Maybe someone with a future or even a present that isn't some kind of existential nightmare.

"I'm gonna fix dinner. You want anything?"

"Nah. I had a few almonds earlier."

I head into the kitchen.

It's Party Pizza time.

13
The Heist

I MAKE IT to work in my car. I forgot to research how to remove the spraypaint from the window so I decide to just let the windshield wipers run continuously and try to wear it away. It's not raining so the squeaking sound is unbearable for the first few minutes of the drive and I have to turn the radio up loud enough to drown it out.

At work, Jolly lies sprawled in the parking lot. He must have lost a bout with one of my co-workers. I imagine Gus as a triumphant victor, standing proudly over Jolly's unconscious body, but when I get into the hut I see Larry Bims, one of the two salesmen who works in the front office, rubbing his hand and looking self-satisfied. His face is flushed and his normally perfectly coiffed hair is slightly askew.

"Congratulations," I say before heading into the filling room.

His self-satisfaction turns into a wide grin and he offers only a quick nod.

Gus isn't there. The only person in the filling room is Diane Marbles. She sits to my right and is usually crying. I don't know anything about her other than that, aside from crying a lot, she listens to books on tape via an old knockoff Walkman she keeps in a fanny pack around her waist, stores a case of Coke under her chair, ritualistically leaves notes on said Cokes warning people not to steal them, and eats a sad sandwich every day for lunch. The sandwich is always wrapped in foil and looks like it contains a single slice of cheese between two pieces of rumpled white bread. I've never been jealous of her sandwich.

I give myself a scratchdown and take a seat at my faucet.

I pull the first bottle from the case to my right, fill it, and place it in the empty case to my left.

I don't know how much longer I can do this. I push the thought away. It's the same thought I've had since about my second hour of working here.

I plug my earbuds into my phone and turn on some electronic ambient music, really loud, to block out the sounds of the running water and Diane's sobs. I wonder if she listens to sad books or if her life is just in ruins.

Gus shows up a few hours later. He taps me on the shoulder and asks if I want to go to lunch. I say "Sure" and we head out to his truck. Following behind him, it looks like he's lost weight.

Jolly's no longer in the parking lot. He's probably in his teepee drinking it off.

We go to the brewery. They don't really have food unless there's a food truck in the parking lot. There isn't so we each get a beer and a large bag of potato chips to split. It's a nice day so we take it out to the deck in back. We're the only ones there.

"I didn't even think this place opened until like four," I say.

"It doesn't," he says. "Tarot works here. They already know me pretty well. There's usually someone here brewing or whatever, I guess."

"Tarot's the girl you met the other day?"

"Yeah. We've been going out. She's pretty cool."

"You look like you've been losing weight."

"Maybe. I don't own a scale or anything. I have noticed something, though."

I take a sip of my beer and wait for him to tell me. He doesn't so I have to ask, "What have you noticed?"

"I'm pretty sure my cock is bigger."

A man runs down the bike path in front of us. He's dragging a rickshaw that contains two children and two dogs. He looks very fit and determined.

"How's that?" I ask.

"I don't know, man. I think it's from being in the Well of Purity."

"You think?"

"I do. Think about it: the raise, meeting Tarot, losing weight, a bigger cock. I think it all comes from the well. I'm hoping it doesn't wear off."

I'd wondered the same thing but hadn't thought about it wearing off.

"I guess just run with it while you can."

"I'm trying. I don't want to think about it wearing off. What if it's one of those things where things go back to being even worse than they were before?"

"It wasn't so bad though, was it?"

He laughs a little. "I guess not if you're used to it. But, come on, I'm an overweight forty-year-old guy who works in a dead end job and lives with his mom. That's pretty fucking bleak."

I guess he's right. My situation probably isn't much better but I don't want to make myself sound that pathetic. I don't want to cast a shadow over his current good fortune.

"I'm thinking of finally moving out though. Tarot still lives with her ex and Mom's not really cool with me bringing girls around and she never leaves so we feel kind of trapped. Eventually we're going to get busted hooking up on the bike path."

"Maybe not."

He takes a big drink of his beer and smiles a little. "You're right. Maybe not. It is kind of fun."

We finish our beers and Gus goes back into the bar and orders a couple more. We sit out on the deck in the sunlight and watch people jog and bike and walk past. After we finish the beers we head back to the campus.

There's a sour taste in my mouth and I'm desperately trying not to dig into my rash.

When I go inside to my station I see the last case of Godwater I filled still sitting there.

I've never stolen anything from Dr. Jolly's. I'm not sure why. I've stolen things from just about every place I've worked, sometimes probably felonious amounts of stuff. Maybe fancy water had just never interested me enough. It's always seemed super boring. But I think about the turn Gus's life has taken and think it can't really hurt.

I pick up the case, find the salesmen distracted in the front office, and head quickly out to my car, hoping I don't run into Jolly on the way.

I put the case in the back seat and pile some of Alice's clothes over it.

I feel like I've won something.

14
Bring On The Metamorphosis!

THERE IS BLOOD all over the bathroom, especially around the toilet but also around the sink and on the mirror.

Alice is in the bedroom, lounging with her laptop and a cigarette.

"Why's there blood all over the bathroom?" I call.

I think she mumbles something but I can't hear what it is so I go to the door of the bedroom.

"What?" I ask.

She stares blankly at me, her earbuds in.

"Huh?" she says.

"Why's there blood all over the bathroom?"

"Period stuff," she says.

By this I assume she means she's on her period. We never have sex when she's on her period, meaning it will be at least a few days before she discovers the red bumps on my dick that she will undoubtedly interpret as herpes and freak out about. Other than that, I know she's had a number of periods since we've been together and I can't recall her being unable to control her blood flow. Maybe she's taken to free bleeding. If so, part of me wishes she'd started it a long time ago. I could have saved a small fortune on tampons.

She takes my confused stare and lack of speech as further questioning and says, "I have this one guy who's really into it, okay? Don't judge. He tipped huge."

"I wasn't judging. Just . . . maybe you could have cleaned it up?"

"That's part of it. He'll pay to watch me do that too. But he likes it when it's hard and crusty. So he's a guaranteed return customer."

The bathtub seems to be mostly clean. That's what I'm most concerned with anyway.

"Was that a case of Godwater you brought in?" she says.

"Uh, yeah."

"Fancy. Bring me a bottle?"

I want to say no, thinking I'm going to need every fluid ounce of magical power it contains, but because I'm a conflict-hating pussy, I just say "Okay" and dutifully retrieve a bottle from the case in the bathroom and present it to her.

"Why's it in the bathroom?"

I'm too lazy to lie. "I'm going to bathe in it."

She glances at me and says, "Can we really afford that?" and this just reinforces my theory that, even though she occasionally looks at me, she has stopped actually seeing me a long time ago. If she ever did in the first place. To her, I am like the outline of a man labeled 'Ryan' and there aren't really any more details than that.

"I stole it," I say, again because it's easier than lying and might make me seem slightly edgy.

She uncorks the bottle and says, "Try not to lose your job, okay? We need it."

I swallow down my anger, deciding I'll probably jerk off while I'm in the tub. Then I think better of it. My semen would only taint the purity of the water, turning it into a cesspool of my mutant unborn.

She takes a sip of the water and makes a gaggy face.

"This is really warm. Not even warm. Hot."

"It's been in the car all day."

"Bring me a glass of ice?"

I want to tell her this defeats the purpose. Pouring hot Godwater over ice just means it's going to be fifty percent Dayton municipal tap water, which cannot be good for you. But I don't care. I go into the kitchen and dutifully retrieve her glass of ice. When I get back to the bedroom, the door is closed and there's a note on it that says, "Plz leeve ousside the dor."

I grimace and set the glass on the shitty laminate floor.

MY HANDS ARE raw and nearly blistered by the time I've uncorked all the bottles, despite the patented E-Z Cork technology, and the bathtub is not nearly as full as I thought it would be.

Still, I'm hopeful.

Look how it had transformed Gus. All I want is a simple rash removed. It doesn't even have to disappear. I just want it to stop itching.

I strip off my clothes and avoid looking in the mirror.

I step into the bathtub. The water comes to just above my ankles and immediately turns a sort of brown-gray from the crud on my feet. I plop down into the water. I'm going to have to flop around in the tub like some sort of swollen, turgid sea mammal just to completely cover myself. How long will I need to stay in here? Gus had stayed in the well nearly all night and had achieved nearly total transformation. I don't know if I need that. I don't want to be too greedy. Still, I'll need to remain in here a few hours at least.

I quickly realize that, as with most things, I've been overly romanticizing this moment.

I'd envisioned myself as being submerged in the waters from the Well of Purity, engulfed by the scent of an earthy spring. Instead, I find myself reclining in a tiny bathtub, the water barely tickling the bottom of my scrotum, engulfed in the scent of menstruation.

Alice comes in every couple of hours to use the bathroom and I silently beg her not to defecate.

15
Dark Fate

SOMEONE HAS SLASHED all the tires on my car.

There is an old photo of Charle taped to each of the hubcaps and another under one of the windshield wipers so I don't have to think too hard about who might have done this.

Bart.

I should be righteously upset, which I kind of am, but quickly look down the street to make sure he's not still around. Fucking with my car is awful, but at least it doesn't physically hurt.

The Monarch regally saunters up to me, a cigarette in his left hand and what looks like a box of wine in his right. He has the car ashtray clipped to his belt like a fanny pack dedicated to lung cancer.

He waves his cigarette at my car and says, "It was that guy in the truck again. I seen him do it. Just got right down and—slash, slash, slash," he pauses, "*slash!*"

He rests the cigarette in the ashtray, tilts his head back, lifts what I'm now sure is a box of wine and depresses the nozzle, unleashing a stream of deep red into his mouth.

"Do you think maybe you could call the cops the next time you see him do something like that?"

Then I have to wonder if getting the cops involved is really something I want to do.

"I woulda," he says, "but my phone's out for repair."

He offers the box of wine to me.

I take it and try mimicking his technique but manage to only get some of it in my mouth while sloshing the rest across my chin and down my shirt.

"Thanks."

"No problem." He casts a glance at the house and says, "We should hang out some time. My boys and I like to have fun."

I'm not a very social person and don't know what fun is but I think about the deafening loneliness of living with Alice and the fact my best friend is becoming someone I resent too much to comfortably hang out with.

I resist the urge to give myself a vigorous scratchdown and say, "Sure. Come by anytime. It's mostly just me and my girlfriend. She works from home a lot so we might have to hang out on the porch but, yeah, I'd be up for it."

"I'll swing by some time." He again gestures at the car with his cigarette and says, "You're in the same boat as me now. I need to find someone who can do tires. I got a stack of em in my yard."

"Let me know if you do."

"I better take off. I gotta couple windows I need to board up."

With that, he takes another healthy swig of wine and turns back toward the other end of the street.

I call Gus to see if he can pick me up.

He sounds groggy.

"Were you still asleep?" I ask.

"Yeah, man, salary."

I'm still not sure he's grasping what this means but what do I know?

"Would you be able to take me to work?"

"Sure, man. It might be a few minutes. Wanna just blow it off? Go get some beers?"

"I really need money right now."

"Okay, man. I'll be there."

I sit on the front porch step and fight the urge to cry.

When did it come to this?

We live in, like, the third saddest neighborhood in Dayton. Looking at it this way seems almost too positive, like there are still a couple of rungs to fall. I briefly think about the time I lived with Callie in Twin Springs. It's something I don't let myself think about that much.

Most of the houses on our street are rentals and maintained to the lowest common denominator of city regulations. This doesn't really bother me too much. If it were up to me, grass and trees and shrubs could take over everything. The more houses I can see, the more depressed I become. With houses come owners—these sad, morbidly obese people wandering out with their tiny yapping dogs, not a single shred of joy or kindness on their faces. And I shrug and try to tell myself it's because they've had rough lives so, due to the fact that I live around them, I am one of them and shouldn't be too judgmental. And if the houses don't have occupants it's because they've been condemned, foreclosed upon, or the owners have died from old age or an overdose so the empty houses themselves are symbolic of the dark fate awaiting people who live here.

I scratch furiously until it burns and dead skin is impacted beneath my fingernails.

It wasn't like Callie and I had any more money when we were living together than I have now. Still, my memories of that time seem bright and happy. I worked at Dr. Jolly's. She worked part-time at both a bookstore and a cafe in the town. She was also a member of Team Klaus. She was Klaus Yellow. Most people who weren't familiar with Team Klaus assumed it was four dudes, but it was actually three women and one man. They toured fairly often and I went along when I could afford to take the time off. I got a lot of writing done when I couldn't go with them. When Callie was home we spent our evenings reading, drinking beer, and watching horror movies and staying up late into the night talking. We spent our days off making good food and hiking the trails surrounding Twin Springs. It felt good. It felt healthy. And I had trouble thinking of another time in my life when I'd been happier.

As with all things, I should have known failure was right around the corner.

Of course it was mostly my fault—okay, it was all my fault—but it was probably my entire life that led up to that extremely poor decision and, while I take full responsibility, I still can't help but think there is some cumulative effect that led to it. Like I'd never really been allowed to be happy and, when finding myself happy, couldn't help freaking out about it.

My life has mostly been a series of lows. Perhaps that's why this current period seems to be particularly brutal, because it follows such a high—possibly the only high point in my life. And I'm so self-loathing I tell myself I should be happy I at least had that couple-year period.

The Cadillac I'd seen parked in front of the house the one day—I was pretty sure it was the same one, not a lot of Cadillacs in the neighborhood—drives by the house and, because it's a dead end, has to conspicuously back into the driveway and go back the way it came.

A few minutes later it stops at the end of one of the perpendicular roads before turning left and continuing away from the house.

I glance over at Mapes's house and his blinds are parted. I can't see him but imagine him in there watching me.

I feel surveilled.

Gus finally shows up what feels like two hours later.

Tarot is in the truck with him.

I open the door and she scoots over. The cab smells like patchouli, cigarette smoke and, maybe, sex.

I'm slightly disappointed Tarot is with him. Not because I have any problems with her. Clearly, my Godwater cure didn't work so I'd thought up an alternate plan and am not sure I want to share it with anyone but Gus.

"Thanks, man," I say as he backs out onto the road. "Hey, Tarot."

"Hey, man," she says. She probably doesn't know my name.

I check the side mirror to see the black Cadillac ominously slide onto my street and park in the driveway.

Alice must be really curious about cable.

"You working today?" I ask Gus.

"Nah. But Tarot has to. She works at Thing. Didn't Callie work there?"

Again I fight the urge to break down and cry and just say, "Yeah. Mason still working there?"

"Sure is," Tarot says.

"Still miserable?"

She laughs a little. "That's Mason. He's all right, I guess."

As with nearly everyone living in Twin Springs, Mason was some form of part-time artist. Or as was the case with most of the people there, a full-time artist who had to do other things to live. Actually, most of the people there either had money or came from money and just identified as artists because it was better than doing nothing. In Mason's case, he was a writer. Unlike me, he had a book on Amazon and everything. Even though he only had one it seemed to have a lot of reviews, meaning people had bought it at some point in time, and this created a lot of jealousy and resentment the few times Callie had forced me to hang out with him. He seemed to be completely blocked after the one book, though, and this made me feel slightly better.

"Well," I say, "those who can't write books sell them, I guess." I can't help myself. I know it's a shitty thing to say.

"Anyway," Gus says, "I was going to look at places around town to rent after I drop you guys off so I'll still be around if you need me to pick you up."

"Cool. Thanks."

I covertly scratch myself, bum a smoke from Gus and, once we're off 675, stare at the rolling green countryside on the way to Twin Springs.

FAILURE AS A WAY OF LIFE

The atmosphere at work is celebratory. In a rematch, Dr. Jolly had knocked Bims out that morning after two rounds and Bill Chappeau, a famous comedian who'd derailed spectacularly in the '90s and chosen to hide in plain sight in Twin Springs, had come in to buy five cases of Godwater.

16
Thinking of the Future

GUS DROPS ME off and Alice isn't here.

I urinate and notice the rash on my cock is even worse. It's worse over my whole body but this is what I focus on.

I have water and a can of beans for dinner.

I sit in my chair and think about how I'm going to break up with Alice. Realistically, I'd like to have sex with her at least one more time but I'm afraid she'll notice the rash and blame me for any future STDs she gets and the rash will only be more noticeable by the time she's off her period. She is even more petty and vindictive than me and I feel like, were she not on her period, she would also want to fuck before breaking up so I know what I'm missing out on. My mind reels. It will probably be the best sex we've ever had. I need to act soon.

I check the balance of my bank account and immediately cancel everything except for gas, electric, water, and my phone.

The lack of an internet connection will fuck with Alice's work but, hopefully, this will just make her more okay with me breaking up with her.

I take a deep, shaky breath and think about doing something I haven't had to do in nearly a decade—ask my dad for money.

I scratch my scalp and a clump of hair falls out.

17
Dad

I call it Dad's house but he doesn't live there alone. He lives with his new wife, Trish. My mom died a few years ago and my dad, a staunch conservative Christian most of his life, became *that* guy—some kind of weird bar hopper, adopting a sort of beachcomber chic aesthetic. I thought he would become a little cooler and more relaxed, but he seems to have become an even bigger asshole.

I imagined what his opening line was—"Hey, baby. I got a timeshare in Clearwater!"

This behavior landed him exactly the type of woman I figured it would—an overly tanned, bleached blond, fake-titted divorcee with five kids of her own. Goodbye inheritance!

I'm not sure why Dad didn't bother finding a woman who actually lived in Florida. Trish wanted to be close to her kids who lived in Ohio so Dad bought a house in Milltown, one of the most depressing cities in the area. Even though it was where he went to high school and had spent a number of his adult years, I still like to think he did it just to be sarcastic. There weren't many good things about Dayton but if you were to strip it of those few decent things, you'd have Milltown.

Gus takes me there. I hope my lack of transportation will increase the sympathy payment I'm in search of.

"This is so cool," Gus says in the truck.

"Seeing my dad is cool?"

"I guess. It's been like nearly twenty years. Wouldn't it be wild if your dad and my mom had hooked up?"

"Wild, maybe. Good? I'm not so sure."

"You don't talk about your dad much."

"He's kind of a dick. You remember. We don't have much in common. Your mom seems nice. I can't really say that about my dad. I mean, he meets the minimal requirements for what is societally acceptable as a decent dad. But that's about it. I don't know. I guess I should consider myself lucky he's not a complete fuck-up. I mean, in the great scheme of things, I'm a way worse dad."

"You probably do okay. I can't even imagine what it would be like. It's not your fault Jen's a psychopath."

"That's what I keep telling myself."

We get to my dad's house. It's in a middle-class section of Milltown so it's not as depressing as it could be. I ring the doorbell. I used to just walk right in but stopped once Trish moved in.

She answers the door.

"Well, hi, Ryan!" She's as friendly as ever. Almost bubbly. Trish is on a lot of really good medication. And also possibly drunk.

"Hey, Trish. Dad around?"

"He's at the shooting range. You can go on down if you want."

"I'll wait."

Dad turned the basement of his house into a shooting range. I'm sure this violates a number of city codes but he's managed to sound-proof it in such a way you can't really hear the shots outside the house.

"C'mon in," she says. She glances almost flirtatiously at Gus and says, "Who's your friend there?"

"Oh, this is Gus. Gus, Trish. Trish . . . Gus."

"Hi Gus." She looks back at me. "Wait till Malinda gets a load of him."

"She around?" I say just to sound polite, to make it sound like I'm interested in seeing her again, which I'm not. All of Trish's kids are horrible.

"She's probably in her room. She's the last one at home."

The other four are busy advancing in their careers as criminals and drug addicts. The ones that aren't already in prison, anyway.

We step into the house, a muffled stream of what sounds like semi-automatic gunfire greeting us.

I imagine Malinda in her room with earphones on, trying to drown out the lunatic downstairs. I'm thankful my father was not retired when I was a teenager. I didn't have to deal with him a lot.

We go inside and sit around the dining table located at the end of the family room. The giant screen TV is on and we all stare hypnotically at it. I think maybe I should go down to the shooting range to talk to Dad. It might be the only chance we'll have to be alone. But I can't. Guns make me anxious and slightly nauseated. It's an irrational fear. I worry some part of my brain is going to think it's a really good idea to point the gun at myself or possibly even someone else and pull the trigger. It's not even really an overwhelming urge. Just the fact it's a possibility is enough.

We watch the TV. It's a reality show called *Drunk and Out of Control*. It centers around a washed up sitcom star from the '90s, his much younger wife, and their two teenage children—one boy and one girl. The arc of this episode is that the father has shit the bed sometime in the course of the evening, the brother and sister blacked out the previous night and are trying to remember if they'd made out or worse, while the harried and intoxicated mother must harangue the bedraggled staff and rustle footage from the security cameras to piece together the events of the previous evening. She's drinking a bottle of chardonnay as the camera zooms into her bronzed and botoxed face and she exclaims, "OMG! Your guys' drinking is making me drink!"

Trish laughs and paraphrases, "You guyses' drinking is making me drink! I love this show. It's so funny."

"It hurts to watch," I say. "They're embarrassing themselves."

"I like it," she says, like her critical stamp of approval should be enough to end the conversation.

"Why?"

"I just do. I can't believe people live like that. They're so crazy."

"It doesn't make you feel dumber?"

She doesn't answer me and I think it's because she doesn't want to acknowledge the truth—she couldn't be any dumber.

I sit there for a few more minutes and feel bad for shitting all over something Trish enjoys. I try to open my mind and see what people can enjoy about it but feel like I'm dying so I get up to use the restroom.

I pee and wash my hands. The spot of missing hair on my head has grown larger and the rash has spread to my left eyelid. Soon, I think, I'll have achieved one-hundred percent coverage. What then? Maybe I'll transform into something, like a superhero.

I head back to the dining area, remembering my plan I need to discuss with Gus.

Malinda is sitting next to Gus, staring nearly open-mouthed at him. Even Trish occasionally looks away from the TV to eye Gus. It's like he's not even the same person he was a couple of weeks ago. He looks like a male model from a magazine, complete with a glossy glow and everything.

"Hey, Malinda." I sit between her and Trish.

"Hey," she mumbles. I don't think she knows my name. I'm guessing when I'm not there it's uttered exactly zero times.

She holds her phone up and takes a picture of Gus.

He glances at her, half-annoyed, and smiles it away with gleaming white teeth.

The show on the TV ends and another one starts up immediately.

Great! A marathon!

The voiceover suggests this episode is going to be about the mother trying to convince the family they don't need to pile into the car and go to Taco Bell at two in the morning. There's a scene of the dad behind the wheel, shouting his order and leaning his head out to vomit. His daughter is bouncing out of the sunroof, her chest blurred, shouting, "Tits out, America!"

Trish does not repeat this line. Just smiles and shakes her head.

I fight the urge to go to the bathroom again. I take a cue from Malinda and Gus and pull out my phone. Of course I haven't missed any texts or anything and, since I don't do social networking, I don't really know what I'm supposed to do with it. I search 'itchy red rash,' click on the images tab, and spend the next several minutes working myself into a low-grade panic attack.

Eventually, Dad emerges from the basement wearing a Make America Great Again t-shirt, a straw panama hat, and yellow shooting glasses.

"Son," he says, "whaddya need?"

All the other eyes around the table turn to me and I feel like the lowest form of life on the planet. I feel small, which means Dad must feel accomplished.

"I just . . . wanted to stop by," I lie.

Dad has spotted Gus and his face lights up. Dad has always been more partial to strangers. I got the feeling he liked all of my high school friends better than me.

"Randy Noman." Dad extends his hand. He doesn't even know it's Gus.

Gus seems taken off-guard by the formality. He stands awkwardly and says, "Gus Brightly." It's been so long since I've heard him use his last name I'd almost forgotten what it was.

Dad seems taken aback. "Well, I didn't even know it was you! Are you a model or something?"

Gus smiles and says, "Fraid not. I work with Ryan."

"You certainly ain't the Gus I remember." Dad's eyes are alight and I can tell he sees in Gus everything he wishes I could be. He turns to me and says, "Still have that girlfriend? What's her name? Annie?"

"Alice."

"Better keep her away from this one." He points a thumb at Gus in an overly comic way.

"She's, uh, she's still around."

"Hear from Charles lately?"

I think about correcting him—it's Charle—but what's the point? Dad's only met Charle twice in the sixteen years he's been around.

I shrug. "He's okay, I guess. He's having some trouble at school—"

"Bring him up here," Dad interrupts. "Get him away from that deadbeat. Raise him right."

I don't have a response to this. I'm baffled that anyone who knows me—even as little as my father knows me—could possibly think I would do an even remotely acceptable job of raising a child.

"Well," Dad says, "we were plannin on goin to dinner. How much you need?"

I lightly scratch my chest and swallow my pride. Who am I really embarrassing myself in front of anyway? Gus knows I'm poor. Dad will never think I don't need money. And Trish and Malinda are, well, they're both sponging off my dad, too. I guess the difference is that they don't have to ask for it. Actually, they probably do. And Dad probably makes them feel as shitty about it as he makes me feel. So maybe their looks are empathy stares.

"Someone slashed the tires on my car. Jen's been pestering me for more money for Charle—"

"Two hundred?" Dad has his wallet in his hand, rifling through it. He refuses to use credit cards and carries garish amounts of cash around with him. He grew up poor. This makes him feel rich. It may be one of the reasons he keeps a gun concealed on him at all times.

"You really don't have to," I say. This is the game we play.

He throws the bills onto the table with a flourish, trying his best to smile affably, but the look in his eye is closer to tears and I wonder if the pain is over departing with the money or because I'm such a colossal failure. Probably both.

I collect the bills and stick them in my pocket.

"Mr. Moneybags," Trish says.

"He's needy," Dad says. "I'm thinkin Wendy's."

"Wendy's is good," Trish says.

Malinda rolls her eyes.

"What do you want? Taco Bell?"

Malinda smiles a little and says, "Yeah," and in that moment I feel incredibly sorry for her.

"Fine. I'll drive you through Taco Bell. We'll just drive all over town until everybody gets what they want. But we're goin there first. I don't want my food gettin cold."

What I want is to get away.

"You ready?" I ask Gus.

He seems slightly confused, like he thought we would be here longer. "Sure," he says. And I remember this is a guy who has movie nights with his mom. He drinks with her. They talk about the same things we talk about. He can never understand. It also probably doesn't occur to him Dad did not ask if we wanted to come along.

Dad probably ate like two hours ago and this is his way of getting rid of us. I show up. He has somewhere he needs to go. It's been that way since Mom died. Dinner is just an excuse. Were I not there, he would never opt to spring for dinner for three, even if it was just shitty fast food value meals.

Gus and I get back in the truck.

"You ever find a place in the Springs?" I ask.

"Yeah," he says. "We found a little house in town."

"Need help moving?"

"Hired movers."

"Fancy."

"I don't have much but Tarot's got a lot of shit."

"You like her, huh?"

"She's cool," he says. "But, you know, we're keeping things open."

"That doesn't . . . make you crazy?"

"No way. It was my idea. Every girlfriend I've ever had has cheated on me. Might as well accept it as an inevitable."

I want to tell him this was before he looked like a Greek god.

"Plus," he adds, "women have been throwing themselves at me left and right. I might as well make the most of it. We'll throw a party when we get settled in."

I tell him my Godwater bath failed, as if it isn't obvious. I propose my new plan to him. He's on board but it'll have to wait until he gets back to work. He's taking a week off to move because salary.

18
It's Not You, It's Me

ALICE LIES IN BED. She has a cigarette in her right hand, a condom on each digit of her left, and is completely naked. Her laptop is closed on the floor next to her and she's staring at the unmoving ceiling fan with a faraway expression.

I plop down next to her, fully clothed.

I take a deep, shaky breath and say, "I don't think this is working out."

I take one of her cigarettes and cradle it.

"What do we do?" she says

"I don't know."

"I'm not moving out."

"Okay."

"I hate you."

"Okay."

"I've hated you for a while."

"I know. At least, I think I knew that. I had a feeling."

"You're super boring. Lazy. Spineless. Average-looking at best." She glances over at me. "No. You're actually somewhat unfortunate looking. I think you were better looking when we first got together.

You've let yourself go. Let's see . . ." She takes a drag from her cigarette and knocks some ash off in the ashtray. "You think you're way smarter than you are."

This type of banter used to constitute foreplay with us but it's different this time. I light the cigarette I'd been rolling around in my fingertips.

"Why now?" she says.

The truth is the sex was the only thing making this remotely worthwhile and now, what with the rash making it an impossibility, it just doesn't feel worth the psychic and emotional strain. But I can't tell her this.

"I think you want something different. I think you deserve better."

"I agree," she says.

I become oddly emotional and choke back tears while I finish my cigarette. She's already put hers out. She balls her bony little hand into a fist and hammers it down on my crotch.

I cough, stave off a wave of nausea, and slink out of the bed.

"I had to," she says.

"I know," I rasp.

"You owe me twenty dollars."

"What?"

"Twenty dollars. You're lucky. That's the friend rate. We're not boyfriend and girlfriend anymore. I just let you lay in bed with me and smoke a cigarette. It was a service. Like cuddling for voyeuristic nihilists."

I reach into my pocket and separate one of the bills from the modest wad.

I place it on top of her laptop and say, "No tip."

19
The Monarch's Kingdom

I SIT IN MY CHAIR and open my laptop. My internet subscription hasn't run out yet. I contemplate browsing for free porn and open up the history to wipe it. The last search performed on the browser was: "how far do i insert fingers in ass to clean it."

I wipe the browser.

I do not search for porn.

I send Gus a text and ask if he wants to go to Easy J's.

He texts back and says he's too busy with the move and I sit in my chair and feel dejected and bored.

I think about using the money I have to replace the tires on my car but wouldn't it just happen again?

I take an envelope, write Jen's address on it, put the money in it, put a stamp on it, and take it to the mailbox.

The Monarch is shuffling around on the sidewalk in front of my house.

"Hey, man," I say.

He makes a sound like "Rarraup" and I realize he's way drunker at this hour than he is in the morning.

"You okay?" I ask.

He shuffles a little way up my walk, gestures wildly with a hand holding a plastic pint bottle of cheap whiskey and says, "I seen that guy. The one."

"Which guy?"

He turns to motion to my car and nearly falls down.

"Oh, that guy. I think I know who it is. I'm trying to get it taken care of."

"Seen him . . . leavin yer house!"

I figure he probably tried to ransack it. He wouldn't have found anything of value.

"See a lotta guys comin and goin. Ol Mapes says she's worth it."

Mapes?

Gross.

I thought the Republican in the Cadillac was bad enough but Mapes would have to be an all-time low. I feel a momentary sense of pride that I had the balls to break up with Alice.

"How's this work?" he says. "I pay you?"

He reaches into his pocket and pulls out money that looks like it's been buried in dirt for a century.

"Put your money away," I say. "It's not like that."

"People around here talk, ya know."

"You need any help getting home?"

He shakily puts the money into his pocket and tries to regain his regal posture.

"I guess I wouldn't mind some company. Got a houseful of people waitin on me."

I was expecting him to say no. Now my vague sense of agoraphobia kicks in and I wish I hadn't made the offer. I've never been beyond my driveway on foot.

The Monarch doesn't walk so well. I don't hold onto his arm or anything because we're not dating, plus he smells kind of weird, like liquor and cigarettes but with some underlying odor like old mushrooms. I walk on the sidewalk. He staggers over the tree space between the sidewalk and the road. At one point he drops to his knees and vomits into someone's yard.

He pulls himself upright, regains his poise, and says, "I feel a lot better now."

We near the end of the street and I'm about to ask him which house is his, but I figure it's the one with all the noise coming from it. It sounds like a house that should be lit up and, as we draw closer, I realize it probably is lit up but, since all the windows are boarded up, a casual observer wouldn't be able to tell.

The Monarch staggers over to a dark-colored car covered in a fuzzy layer of mold, pats the trunk, and says, "Here she is. The old Monte Carlo."

All four tires are flat and I think that, probably, the last good year the Monarch had was maybe 1986.

"Well, let's go in and meet the boys."

We walk up the few steps of the Monarch's porch and now, so close to the house, it's easy to tell where his underlying odor comes from— the toxic-looking black mold covering his front door, the outside of his house and, probably, I'm just guessing, the inside as well.

Not that you can tell.

Because as we enter the house, there isn't a single surface of wall that's visible. Hardly any of the ceiling. Definitely none of the floor.

Goat paths of compressed trash run through shelves teetering with books and records and less identifiable junk. This house is probably twice the size as the one I'm renting and the amount of shit stuffed into it is astounding. There are lights on in the house but the moldering heaps around us have a way of dampening them.

"The boys are probably out back," the Monarch says. "They say it feels too tight in here for em."

We take the goat path through the first room and enter what I suspect is the kitchen, mainly because of the table that has a mountain of old newspapers stacked to the ceiling and a collection of old plastic shopping bags stuffed under it. The back door at the far end of the kitchen is open, hanging by one hinge.

The Monarch inspects the disconnected hinge and says, "I'm gonna have to get that fixed."

We descend the back porch steps into an overgrown backyard lit by a yellow security lamp.

A vine-choked, moldy wooden privacy fence runs around the perimeter of the backyard. It's missing a number of slats and leans into the yard. I imagine the Monarch's entire lot just one day falling in on itself and sinking into the earth, an instant landfill.

The Monarch leads me back to the garage. The door is propped open with 2x4s. Two boys who look twelve or thirteen sit on an old couch and work the controls for a video game on a large screen TV. They're chubby and doughy looking, wearing ball caps, logo t-shirts, sweatpants, and puffy tennis shoes.

"Pete and Chab," the Monarch says.

Two other boys, maybe a little older but dressed pretty much the same, are farther back in the garage, standing in a circular clearing. They each take a drink from a tall can of beer and set the beers on the floor. Then they face off, the boy on the right drawing back his hand and slapping the boy on the left so hard his hat flies off. I wonder what the point of this is until I notice the phone on a tripod, recording the antics, and think, "Views." That's the point, I guess.

"Beer's in the barrel over there." The Monarch gestures toward a rusty industrial drum.

I wonder if drinking anything that comes from that will give me tetanus or possibly even a weirder, more lethal disease but decide to throw caution to the wind. It's been a few days since I've had a beer and my finances are in no state to turn down anything free.

I grab a beer and crack it open.

"Them's Landon and Tyler," the Monarch says. "They're tryin to get famous. They got a MeTube series called *Drink and Slap*." He pauses. "The title pretty much says it all. It ain't too subtle."

The Monarch strolls over to a beaten, lopsided recliner in a shadowy corner of the garage and collapses into it. I grab an old paint bucket and sit down on it.

The Monarch slits his eyes and stares at the two boys on the couch.

"The boys been comin over most nights for the past couple years. Sometimes they don't all come. Sometimes they bring they're friends and I have a real houseful. I used to have about twelve cats but they all run off. Still got a dog around here someplace. That tall one there," he waves his whiskey bottle toward one of the upright boys, "Landon, he's got a lot of brains. He's already got his GED and everything. He's the one put the idea together for the TV series. I think he's really gonna make somethin of himself. Now Tyler just does everything Landon tells him. If he just listens to him and doesn't get too full of himself, he'll probably get to go along for the ride. But he's already been in juvie a couple of times and'll probably end up in jail as soon as he's not a minor."

A loud concussive boom shakes the garage. No one acknowledges it.

As soon as I can gain my bearings, I say, "What the hell was that?"

"I figure there are three possibilities." The Monarch holds up two fingers. "Probably Wright-Patt. It's all top secret shit, right? And they're always testin out new stuff the public ain't allowed to know about. The second reason might be someone's meth lab blew up but you don't hear about that as much as you used to. I think people mostly do heroin around here now. Makes sense. Can't really sleep on meth. It's like, uh . . . multiplyin the misery. Ain't nobody around here wants to make his life three times longer than it is. Heroin lets you just drift away and forget about things for a while. And it's pretty cheap right now."

The Monarch falls silent and I imagine him thinking about heroin.

"What's the third thing?" I ask.

"Oh," he says. "That might be Wilmot next door. He's one of them . . . What do you call the black guys with dreadlocks and shit?"

"Rastafarian?"

"Yeah, he's one of them. Anyway, he has this big ol shotgun he likes to come out and wave around when he's had too much to drink. Keeps sayin he's gonna blow his head off. Maybe he finally went and did it."

"Should I, uh, call somebody?"

"Wouldn't do no good now, would it? Drink your beer. Get loose. Have a good time."

I'm pretty sure I'm way too on edge to do that, even though I know it's exactly what I need.

"Now them two boys there on the couch, I'm pretty sure they're retarded or something." He laughs a little. "They'll set and play that game till they fall asleep. I usually gotta wake em up and send em home."

I drink as much beer as I can as fast as I can.

The Monarch talks. I mostly listen.

He tells me how he used to work at a machine shop until getting laid off in the late '90s. He talks about everything he wants to do: start a halfway house, convert his garage into a morgue because the county morgue has reached maximum capacity what with all the overdoses, start a food truck that sells sandwiches and cigarettes for the after bar crowd, get his car fixed, rent a storage space, get his house fixed, use his house as a storage place for other people for a small fee, maybe move somewhere where it's warm all year long, buy up all the houses in the area so he can have a compound, and maybe start going to church.

Once they finish slapping each other, both of their faces bright red, Landon and Tyler stand around and drink and scroll through their phones.

The Monarch seems to drift off while talking.

I keep drinking, watching the other guys in the garage. I don't talk to them and they don't talk to me.

The Monarch snaps awake after a little while. He springs toward the boys on the couch and starts smacking one of them on the head.

"Everybody needs to get on home now!" he shouts. "Just get the hell away from me!'"

I join the boys as we run through the backyard and out to the sidewalk. They're all laughing. I'm slightly horrified.

"Crazy old bastard," Landon says.

"The Monarch's too awesome," one of the younger ones says.

I head back to my house and they go in the opposite direction.

I get home and forget I've broken up with Alice. The bedroom door is closed but I can see the light is on. There's laughing and sex noises coming from the room.

I turn off the living room light and collapse onto the couch, asleep within a few minutes. Thank god for the beers.

20
Calls From the Past

I'M IN THE KITCHEN, staring out at the overgrown backyard, eating crackers and drinking water, and thinking I really need to go to the store.

My phone vibrates with a text.

It's from Jen.

"Bart says the first installment has been made. I'll need more in a week."

I just put the money in the mail last night. I didn't even know if it had run yet today. There's no way she would have already received it.

Something else flashes through my mind.

The noises coming from the bedroom last night.

Did Alice . . .?

Then I have another thought.

I walk through the house and to the mailbox.

Damn. It's gone.

Maybe Bart just took it out of the mailbox. Maybe that's what Jen meant. Somehow that feels more comfortable than my ex-girlfriend giving freebies to my ex-brother-in-law to save me from further repercussion. I dismiss the thought. There's no way Alice would do that.

I go back into the kitchen and finish my crackers, pulling my phone out to stare blankly at it.

I'd overlooked the missed call and voicemail received before Jen's message. It must have come in while I was sleeping or brushing my teeth or something.

It's from the unknown number.

I listen to the voicemail.

I hear nothing.

I imagine a sun-blasted bone white facade, the kind that hang onto the sides of mountains overlooking a sparkling blue sea in someplace like Greece. I imagine the warm breeze rippling the curtains as the caller stares out at the sea, waiting to talk and never saying anything.

I feel a surprising lightness in my soul and a heaviness in my heart.

This caller, she's been there all along, and I'd been too blind to realize who it was. Or, at least, who I want it to be.

Callie.

Where is Callie these days? I wonder.

I know she isn't in Twin Springs. She didn't come back from the last tour I'd accompanied her on.

Team Klaus is spread around the United States. One lives in Vermont. One lives in Austin. One in Portland.

They pass their files around until they have an album's worth of stuff and then tour together.

I imagine Callie is in one of those places.

She doesn't do social networking. She changed her phone number after I . . . after we split up.

I imagine seeking her out. I imagine showing up with a magic bag filled with a world of apologies, begging her to take me back.

A portly guy who looks about fifty, balding and disheveled, wearing a white wife beater and blue boxers, wanders into the kitchen.

"Scuse me," he says.

He grabs a glass from the cabinet and runs some water in it, taking a huge, satisfying gulp.

He looks at me and says, "Marshall," holding out a hand that has probably been in Alice.

"Ryan." I extend my hand.

He quickly glances me up and down and says, "Is that contagious?"

"I don't think so."

"What is it?"

"I don't know."

"You should get that looked at."

"I know."

And I wonder if I will if my plan doesn't work out.

"I gotta get my clothes on and get back to work. Nice meeting you."

After he leaves, Alice comes into the kitchen wearing a small white t-shirt and black underwear. I feel myself getting hard and try not to look at her or at least focus on her face. She looks tired.

"Cam stuff was a lot easier," she says. "Thanks a lot for shutting the internet off."

"I can't afford it."

She opens one of the cabinets.

"Did you already eat?"

"I had some crackers. I need to go to the store." As a test, I say, "Rent's due on the first."

She leans against the counter, lights a cigarette and says, "I'm not paying to live here. College is, like, really expensive."

I quickly look her up and down, trying not to seem too thirsty.

"When was the last time you went to class?"

"I still have to pay for it."

I go into the bathroom and jerk off. The rash makes it slightly uncomfortable but, oddly, this makes it more pleasurable. It doesn't take me long and my penis feels raw and burning when I'm finished, which isn't pleasurable at all.

When I go back into the living room, Alice is at least wearing shorts and I feel like the crisis has been momentarily averted.

91

21
Diane Marbles

I TEXT GUS to see if he can take me to work. I wait for a half hour and he never responds. I really need to go to work. I need the money. I remember a co-worker call sheet Dr. Jolly prints out and gives to us a couple of times a year. It's mostly in case the campus is closed due to weather. Dr. Jolly calls the first person on the list and they're supposed to call the next one and so forth. I don't know that anyone uses it for rideshare purposes or not.

Most of the people on the list work in different areas and I don't really know who they are.

In my embrace of failure, my eyes fall to the one person I'd least like to share a ride with—Diane Marbles.

I tap out her number.

"Hello." She sounds so sad that I get momentarily hopeful thinking she probably lives in Dayton too.

"Hi Diane. This is Ryan from work."

"Ryan?"

"Yeah."

"Which one are you?"

"I work in the filling room with you."

"Are you the handsome guy?"

"No. I'm the other one."

"Oh." She sounds more disappointed than she normally sounds.

"Anyway, I was wondering if it would be possible for you to give me a ride to work today. I could pay you for your time and gas. It's only temporary."

There's a long pause. "Where do you live?"

I give her my address.

"I guess it's kind of on my way. Twenty-five sound good?"

Twenty-five sounds like a whole lot but I say, "Sure."

"I'll be there in a little bit."

"Thanks a lot."

I think about asking Alice for the money but she's still in bed and I'm sure she would say no and her purse is probably hanging in the closet anyway.

I open her purse.

There must be thousands of dollars in it. I take the twenty-five and think about taking more but refrain.

I momentarily think about disappearing. It's not my job to take care of Alice and she has more than enough to take care of herself.

What if I did that?

What if I just didn't come back?

Where would I go?

I know where I would go. Well, if I don't know the exact location, I know who I would go to.

Stupid, stupid, stupid, I tell myself.

I open the blinds for the front windows of the house and listen to the last unknown voicemail repeatedly until I see a blue Volvo station wagon pull into the driveway and figure it must be Diane Marbles.

I go out and get in her car, saying thanks before the stench in the car renders speech impossible.

I hear mewling come from the back of the car and look over my shoulder, now realizing why the car smells like a litter box.

It's because it is, basically, a litter box.

There are three cats in the back of the car. The floorboards are full of litter. I roll down my window and stick my head out as Diane starts down the street. The window comes back up and I pull my head back into the car before I'm decapitated.

"I'm afraid they'll get out."

"Maybe just a crack," I wheeze.

"They don't like the wind."

I guess this explains why Diane always parks in a shady part of the parking lot. Probably leaves the car running with the air conditioner on all day too. Maybe that's why she's charging me twenty-five bucks. It seems like it would be cheaper for her to get on disability for whatever mental disorder she has and stay home.

"These are a few of my little guys," she says. She rattles off their names but I'm not paying much attention. It feels like my lungs are slowly shutting down and my eyes and throat itch furiously.

"They like the car. I like to cuddle with them on my breaks. It relaxes me. Makes me feel good."

I wheeze out some unintelligible response, already dreading the ride home.

"When's handsome guy coming back?"

"Next week, I think."

"He just started, didn't he?"

"No. It's Gus. He's been there about ten years."

"Hm," she says. "I don't remember him. How long have you been there?"

"About ten years too. We were both there when you started."

"Hm," she says again, like maybe I'm lying. "Mind if I listen to my tapes?"

"I don't care."

She presses a cassette into the player and the narrator of an audiobook fills the car. Whenever I saw her reading an actual book, they always looked like really mainstream things. This doesn't seem like an exception. From what I can gather of the plot on our trip to the campus, it seems to be about a group of female detectives—ethnically diverse in a weird, pandering way—who solve murders before gathering together to exchange really vanilla-sounding sex advice and quick healthy recipes for the woman on the go. My eyes fall to Diane's sad sandwich in the change console beneath the stereo.

I slide into an allergic fog and continue listening to the audiobook.

As soon as she pulls into a parking space, I'm out of the car.

I hear Diane say, "I'm gonna stay out here and cry a bit," before I slam the door.

I sneeze all the way to the front door of the hut and scratch myself vigorously. There's no way I can ride home with Diane. I'll have to find another way. I regret not taking more money from Alice so I could have gotten an Uber or a cab or just stayed at the motel at the edge of Twin Springs.

Around lunchtime, Dr. Jolly wanders up behind me and says, "It's time."

I'm dazed and listening to some soothing electronic music. I can usually hear what people say even with the earbuds in, but have become so accustomed to ignoring them I don't respond to Dr. Jolly.

He taps me on the shoulder, the standard action taken if whoever is speaking to me actually needs a response.

I pull the earbud out of my left ear and say, "Huh?"

"It's time," he repeats.

"Time for what?"

"You know."

There's an intensity in his eyes that isn't normally there.

"I really don't." I glance at the cases of empty bottles in front of me. "I've got all these bottles to fill."

"It can wait," he says. "Everything can wait."

Up until this point, I didn't know whether to feel lucky or left out. Dr. Jolly has never challenged me to a fight. I've always assumed this is because I'm easily overlooked.

He challenged Gus to a fight shortly after we started there. Gus made it all the way to the parking lot before shitting himself. Dr. Jolly looked disgusted and announced that the match was postponed. Gus said the soiling was intentional but I wasn't entirely convinced. Dr. Jolly hasn't challenged him since.

"I'm in no condition," I say. "Look at me."

He doesn't. Not really.

"You look young and healthy."

"I'm over forty and I hurt all the time. Not to mention this rash. It might be contagious."

"It's just from lack of hygiene."

Nothing I can say will convince him otherwise.

Maybe, at the very least, I can find a way to parlay this into a ride home.

"Meet me in the parking lot," he says before turning to leave.

I take a deep breath and make my way through the office. It's filled with a sense of anticipation. Fresh off his victory over Bims, no one really knows what to expect. It never occurs to me to actually try to win. I've never been in a fight before and shrink from almost all forms of conflict. I wonder if victory would come with some form of bonus. Maybe this is what it takes to get a raise from Dr. Jolly.

I walk out into the hot parking lot and the rest of the office follows me.

Jolly stands in the middle of the parking lot, wearing a Grateful Dead t-shirt and warm-up pants.

I walk up to him and take a half-hearted swipe at his face. He pulls back to easily avoid it and throws a right that hits my cheek. It's not a particularly hard hit and only hurts a little. Nevertheless, I immediately fall to the ground because I don't want to absorb any more of his blows.

Bims rushes up and begins counting to ten. I look at him like, "What's the point?" but he continues anyway.

Jolly stands over top of me and when Bims reaches ten, Jolly says,

"Pathetic," and the rest of the office follows him inside wrapped in collective disappointment.

After a while I stand and make my way back to the office. Jolly is still there, accepting the congratulations, the office staff already talking about the fight as though it were a nearly epic, mythic battle. Pretty standard.

"My vision's blurred," I tell Jolly. "Do you think you'd be able to give me a ride home?"

"I don't drive. It's terrible for the planet," he says. "Who can give the loser a ride home!" He shouts at the rest of the office.

"I can," Diane says. "I already know where he lives."

Great, I think. Now everyone probably thinks we're dating.

"This woman can do it," Jolly says. "Problem solved."

He claps me on the back and I drift back to my workstation. The only thing to be remotely happy about is that I don't have to pretend to be blind for the rest of the day.

22
The Boarder

"Do you know who that guy is?" Alice stands in the kitchen, staring out the window.

I move next to her and follow her line of sight to the porch attached to the garage. I don't know why it isn't attached to the house like most porches but, this way, the garage forms a barrier between us and Mapes, which is good, because the sight of him depresses me more than I already am.

"That's the Monarch," I say.

"He's been out there for a couple of hours."

"I'll go talk to him."

I walk out of the house and go sit next to him on the porch.

"What's up?" I say.

"I'm gonna need a place to stay for a couple of days," he says.

My first thought is: you can't stay here. My next thought is: what makes you think you can stay here? My next thought is: that will probably really piss Alice off.

So I say, "Okay. What's going on?"

"I'm afraid my home has been condemned. This morning I came back from the store. Signs all over it."

"That sucks, man. You're welcome to crash on the couch."

He nods, lights a cigarette, and takes an elegant swig from his forty of cheap beer.

"I can probably just stay right out here. I don't want to cause any tension."

"With her?" I say. "We're just roommates."

"I like it outside. The porch'll be fine."

Maybe he's just trying to ease into homelessness.

"All right, man," I say. "I'm gonna go in and grab some dinner. You hungry?"

"I'm good." He takes another drink of beer and another drag from his cigarette.

Once in the house, I tell Alice the Monarch is going to be staying on the porch for a while.

"Who is he?" she says.

"A guy from the neighborhood."

"How did you meet him? I didn't think you left the house except to go to work."

"I met him . . ." I don't say where I met him. Don't feel the need. I just conclude with, "the other night."

"As long as he doesn't interfere with my job. By the way, I'm missing twenty-five dollars. Do you know what happened to it?"

"I had to pay someone to give me a ride to work."

"When are you going to pay me back?"

I wasn't really planning on it but, then again, I didn't think she'd ever notice.

"Probably when you start paying rent."

"You get paid this Friday, right? You can pay me back then. Rent?" she scoffs. "You should be paying me to live here."

"Whatever."

23
Condemned

I'M NOT SURE why the Monarch is squatting in plain view in the back-yard to shit. There's nothing but woods behind our house. He could have ducked in there if he needed some privacy. Still, there's some-thing very pitiable about an oldish man being forced to shit outside.

Maybe I can catch him in time.

I go out to the yard.

"Monarch!" I call. "You can use the—"

"Too late," he grunts.

I turn before I can see it and call over my shoulder, "Next time!"

In the house, Alice is awake. She's at the table with a glass of ice wa-ter and three orange Tic Tacs.

"You really need to get some groceries. What did you have for breakfast?"

"Coffee."

"We have coffee?"

"It was the last of it."

"Damn."

"There's a store within walking distance. And there are, like, three gas stations."

"I'll just have somebody bring me something."

"You're not going to fuck someone for food, are you?"

"Don't be so crass."

"If the Monarch asks to come in, let him, okay?"

"Who's the Monarch?"

"Our boarder. Well, my second boarder. You're the first. He just shit in the yard. Mapes'll call the city if he catches him."

"We need a second bathroom."

"Maybe if you paid rent I wouldn't need a second boarder."

"So he's paying you?"

"He will. I think."

"You're pathetic."

After she says this my phone vibrates with a text from Jen. It says exactly the same thing: "You're pathetic." But then there's an added: "Second installment is due by the end of next week."

I text back: "Did you get the money I sent?"

She doesn't respond right away so I slide the phone back into my pocket.

"I'm gonna go out and wait for Diane Marbles."

"When are you gonna get the car fixed?"

"Probably never."

I go back outside. The Monarch is casually strolling toward the end of the driveway.

"Where ya going?" I say.

"Gotta go check out the house. Then I'm goin to the station for some libations."

"I'll go with you." I'm curious to see what a condemned house looks like, even though there are plenty of them around. I want to be able to connect the owner to the property. "How was the porch?"

"Okay," he says. "I had a confrontation with a possum on toward dawn. Seen a coyote."

"You really can sleep on the couch if you want."

"I'd rather not. I've entered the Phase." I capitalized this in my head, turned it into some kind of proper noun.

"The Phase?"

"The Third Phase of my life. Maybe the fourth. Some of them are blurry. Anyway, it's the phase where everything falls away." He pauses. "Quite honestly, I'm not sure if I'm ready for it. I think it's some spiritual Buddhist shit or somethin."

He lights a cigarette and offers me one. I take it, hoping it will deaden my sense of smell for the atrocious ride in Diane's car.

We reach his house and stare at it for a few minutes, still smoking.

"I don't think your house is really condemned," I say.

He points with his cigarette and says, "Signs all over."

There are pieces of posterboard with the word 'condemmed' written in what looks like red marker.

"I don't think those are, like, official signs. 'Condemned' isn't even spelled right."

He smiles a little and tosses his cigarette out into the road. "Whooo!" he calls. "The boys are up to their hijinks again. I think they got me this time."

"I better get back to the house before my ride gets there."

"I'll see if I can't get someone to look at your car for you."

"That's all right. I can't pay anybody for a while."

"I'll take care of it. For last night." He looks back at the house and shakes his head in a they-really-got-me way. "Hopefully I won't be needin it again."

"If so then thanks in advance. If not, it's really no big deal. See ya."

I turn and head back home.

Diane Marbles pulls up a few minutes later. She seems even more depressed than usual.

She gets out of the car. I'm confused.

"You're driving," she says.

I don't argue. I don't have any money to pay her today and hope she'll let it slide.

I get behind the wheel.

She flops down on the back seat and soon there are three or maybe even four cats on her and I'm pulling out on my street and she's laughing like a lunatic and by the time we get to work she says the day's too beautiful to work and she's just going to sit in the car and play with her cats and eat her sandwich.

I shrug and go to work.

She asks if I'll bring her two Cokes from under her chair.

24
Not A Party Person

"WHO ARE ALL these people?" I ask Gus.

"Friends," he says. "People I've met at the bar and around town."

"Remember a few weeks ago when I was your only friend?"

He smiles and playfully jabs at my shoulder. "You're still my best friend, man."

We're standing by a table covered in food. I'm currently holding a stack of cheese, crackers, and some kind of smoked meat in my hand, mechanically feeding it into my mouth because I don't know when I'll have the chance to eat this well again. There's booze here too so I'm planning on hitting that pretty hard. Rarely has blacking out been an objective of mine but, at this point, almost anything is better than going home.

"It's funny, man," Gus says. "I always thought I never had any friends because I hated people. But it just turns out that I never really had the time or money to make friends."

I'm looking around at the room of strangers, drinking free booze and eating free food, and wonder if Gus has made friends or bought them.

"Where's Alice?" Gus asks.

"We broke up."

"Really?"

"Yep."

"Shit, man. You should have called or something."

"It's all right. I broke up with her. She still lives there."

"Well, man, I gotta go mingle." Gus rolls his eyes. "Gotta play the good host, ya know?"

Actually, I don't know. Don't have any idea. I would struggle to think of a time I had more than four people in any place I've ever lived.

"We still on for Monday?"

He claps me on the shoulder, "I'll be there, man."

"Think you could pick me up for work too. I've been riding in with Diane Marbles and—"

But he's already walking away, into the roomful of people. I'm pretty sure me and Gus are the oldest people in the room. Of course, if the same water feeding into Dr. Jolly's well is the same water the people of Twin Springs drink, it's entirely possible they've just found some fountain of youth.

I find the beer. There are a few kegs from the local brewery and I fill my plastic cup up several times, taking it to go stand in a corner and people watch. My people watching includes ogling a number of girls. It's warm outside and it seems like a lot of them aren't wearing very many clothes. The state of my penis removes the enjoyment I derive from this act. I fill my cup again. I've lost count how many beers this makes but I'm definitely starting to feel it, so it's been more than a few. I find Gus to bum a cigarette and take it out to his backyard.

Mason Becker, Callie's co-worker at Thing Books, is out there. So maybe me and Gus aren't the oldest people here. It takes me just a second to verify that it is Mason. He's thinner than I remember. Even though he's balding, he now has his hair pulled back into a ridiculous man bun. Maybe he won't try talking to me if I don't approach him. I know what he's going to want to talk about. Either writing or Callie, both of which are painful.

I light the cigarette and breathe it in, focus on the evening insect sounds and the laughter and faint music coming from inside the house.

"Ryan?"

Shit. Mason's now standing next to me. I think about doing the dick thing where I pretend not to remember his name but decide not to.

"Hey, Mason," I say. "I wasn't sure if that was you or not."

"It's been, what? Two years?"

"Bout that."

"Still writing?"

"Nope."

"Me either. Fuck it, right? Ever hear from Callie?"

It didn't take him long to get there at all.

I take a drag from the cigarette before answering him. Along with the smoke, nausea hits me like a truck and I flick the cigarette out into the backyard and drop to my knees, heaving up everything into the grass.

While I'm vomiting, I'm pretty sure Mason is still talking to me like nothing out of the ordinary is happening.

"She's coming around pretty soon. This girl I know started touring with them. I still stalk her MyFace page even though I hate the social networking thing. They're playing in Dayton soon, I think. Or maybe it's Cincinnati. I don't know. I guess I could check my phone but I'm too lazy right now. Well, good to see you, man."

It's been a while since I've thrown up from drinking and I haven't really drunk that much, so maybe that's not it. Maybe the party food sat out too long or had been touched by too many questionable people. Sometimes vomiting makes me feel better, but not this time. I feel completely enervated.

I crawl through my puke, deeper into the backyard, away from the lights of the house.

I roll over onto my stomach and lay my head on my arm.

I'm passing out way earlier than I thought I would, completely over-

shooting my modest goal of a good blackout.
Rather than try to fight it, I just submit.
It feels oddly relaxing.

25
A Brief Vacation

THE MORNING SUNLIGHT is intense. At least, I'm pretty sure it's morning. I'm really disoriented. I realize I'm outside and last night comes back to me with a burst of clarity. I smile and fight the urge to laugh a little. I guess this is one way of getting out of a party. I pull my phone out of my pocket and check the time.

9:37

There are no texts.

I briefly panic until I remember today is Saturday and I don't have to sit on my front porch and wait for Diane Marbles to pick me up for work.

I feel like shit because I always feel like shit but, on the whole, I feel way better than I thought I would. Almost refreshed.

I do not smell very good, though. Probably because of the vomit crusted in my beard.

I sit up and survey the backyard. It's a nice backyard, surrounded by a wooden privacy fence that has all of its boards. This makes me feel a lot less embarrassed.

For a second I panic and wonder how I'm going to get home and then decide not to worry about it. What do I need to get home for? I fight the urge to text Alice and tell her I'm never coming back but ultimately stop myself when I realize that would be an egotistical act and nothing more. She probably would not even notice—much less care—if I didn't come home.

I stand up and wander to the garden hose attached to the back of the house. I survey my surroundings and, since no one is actively staring at me, quickly remove my clothes. I unspool the hose and turn the water on. I spray some hose water into my mouth and swish it around, remembering how much I loved to drink hose water as a child. Might explain why I'm brain damaged now. I rinse my beard thoroughly and spray off the rest of my body, paying particular attention to my balls and my asshole. My t-shirt seems fine and puke free. My jeans, not so much. I spray them with the hose and wring them out. My button-down shirt seems to have gotten the brunt of the puke. It's a lost cause. I turn it inside out and use it as a towel to dry off with. I put my socks, jeans, and t-shirt back on, ball up the button-down and my underwear, find the trashcan and throw them away.

I check my bank account to make sure I got paid yesterday.

I did. Even though Dr. Jolly seems to be doing well, I still wait for some future time when he can't manage to pay anyone or, more likely, just forgets. The drinking and the boxing has to lead to some form of mental trauma eventually.

It's a beautiful morning so I wander into town and get coffee and breakfast from the market since all the restaurants are overcrowded. I eat the breakfast on a bench, watching groups of mostly happy people. I throw my trash away and administer a furious scratchdown. A couple of the patches burst open and begin bleeding. I go back into the grocery store to buy a bottle of water and a pack of cigarettes. Bill Chappeau is in front of me, also buying a pack of cigarettes. I imagine him saying, "Give me all the cigarettes! I'm rich, bee-yotch!" but he only buys one pack before darting out of the store before anyone can stop him to tell him what a big fan they are and how much they like him. He's mastered the art of avoiding the paparazzi by living somewhere

109

that doesn't have the paparazzi. The common sense is staggering.

I take my water and smokes and head to the trails of the nature reserve. I always think this seems like a good idea but after about a half hour of walking I'm reminded of how out of shape and lazy I am and end up sitting on various rocks and benches watching people who are far more driven and athletic than me. I imagine everyone with bright red rashes and bald patches and it makes it more entertaining.

A storm comes up in the afternoon and I make my way back to Gus's. He isn't there so I sit on his porch. When he and Tarot and another girl who looks like she just escaped from a cult show up, I convince him I should just stay here tonight and tomorrow so he doesn't have to come all the way to Dayton to pick me up on Monday morning.

The next two nights are reasonably blissful compared to my agoraphobic hate-filled existence in Dayton. The only real irritant is the girl, whose name is Fee, who has, in fact, recently escaped from a cult. She seems twitchy and overly chatty, like she's just ecstatic to be in the presence of people who do not want to take control of her mind before using her for breeding purposes, i.e. fucking her.

Preparing for a shower that Sunday night, I strip down and look in the mirror, taking stock of the rash.

It's really bad.

I decide to experiment with something I haven't used in a very long time, possibly forever—positive thinking.

It's entirely possible the rash could be gone tomorrow if Gus's and my plan is executed properly.

No. I stop myself. Not 'if.' 'When.' *When* Gus's and my plan is executed properly.

And it's not 'entirely possible' the rash will be gone.

The rash *will* be gone.

I'll be a new man.

Tomorrow.

I take a deep breath and hate stare at the creature in the mirror.

The failure.

The Failure.
"This is your last day on earth," I mutter.
Taking my shower, I think about that guy in the mirror.
I already kind of miss him.

26
A Failure's Baptism

"WHAT IF HE doesn't want to?" Gus says.

"Are you kidding?" I say. "He'll think just the way you look is an attempt to establish male dominance. I'm going to say he challenges you within five minutes."

"What if I don't win? I'm not much of a fighter."

I let this hang in the air of the truck before we both start laughing.

"What if you don't win . . ." I say sarcastically. "C'mon now."

I point to the gas gauge of his truck. It's below empty.

"I mean, do you even remember the last time you put gas in this thing?"

He pretends to think for a minute and says, "Before."

It's all he needs to say. When Gus looks back on his life, there are only going to be two periods. Before and After. Like Christ.

I tap the glass of his rear window, another recent development.

"And when did you pay to get the bag replaced?"

"It just . . . happened."

"And how much are you paying in rent?"

He's quiet.

"C'mon. How much? It's a nice place in a really desirable area."

"Nothing. I just have to, you know, mow grass and do basic mainte-
nance and stuff."

"And do you think you're ever going to have to do that?"

He sighs. "Probably not."

"Face it. You've won some kind of karmic lottery. And, further-
more, you have the ability to make the most of it. Some people might
freak out about it."

"Are you gonna freak out about it?"

I fight the urge to say, "It's never going to work for me."

Think positive.

"No," I say. "I'm ready."

"Okay then. Let's do this shit."

We walk into the office and then the filling room.

Diane Marbles swivels in her chair, plucks her old wire headphones
from her head, and says, "I knew it was going to be a great day." She's
smiling, something I've never seen her do when not in the presence of
her cats. She looks psychotic. "I made three sandwiches. I haven't had
a three sandwich day in . . . gosh, I don't know if I've *ever* had a three
sandwich day." She looks at Gus the entire time, not even acknowl-
edging me, her rideshare buddy.

I look at the desk behind her. There they are. Three sad sandwiches
individually wrapped in foil resting atop a self-help paperback: *Failure
As a Way of Life*. With my new positive mindset, I think this sounds
horribly defeatist.

I sit down at my faucet, put in my earbuds, and get to work.

Gus sits down at his faucet, covered in dust, fills one bottle, says,
"Mind numbing," and gets up to go wander through the office.

I try not to think about anything. I set about filling the bottles with
great rapidity, inserting the E-Z Cork and placing them in the case to
my left. I feel amazingly light and at ease. I'm not even going to turn
around to check on Gus's progress or to see if Dr. Jolly is in the building. I'll know if it happens. I'll feel it.

And here it is.

I check my phone.

So it's been a little longer than five minutes. Maybe I would have lost that bet.

The collective wave of excitement reaches into me and, for the first time, I actually feel it. The excitement. Normally I just feel irritated and put out that I have to stand up and walk outside to watch two idiots punch each other. But, other than the overall feel of the office after such an event, I've never really had much of a stake in this.

Today, however, the stakes are very high.

My future depends on what happens in the parking lot.

I follow my co-workers out. Diane Marbles has a sandwich in her hand. Early lunch.

Gus and Dr. Jolly square off in the parking lot.

We all gather around them.

Jolly strips off his shirt and bounces from Converse to Converse.

Gus just kind of stands there, squinting.

Jolly bounds toward Gus and Gus says, "I'm so sorry," before leveling him with a right to the chin.

Gus hangs his head.

Bims stands over Jolly's prone body and counts to ten. Everyone erupts in claps and cheers. This has never happened before. Jolly has been knocked out before—although probably never with one blow—but no one has ever cheered when he's been defeated. Usually, there's the feeling the rest of the office might turn feral and pounce upon the victor, ripping him to pieces.

People approach Gus, clapping him on the back and ruffling his hair like some of his magic will rub off on them. Or maybe it's just to feel those golden, silky tresses.

Gus affably accepts their congratulations but, after a few minutes, says, "Okay, everybody can go back in. I'll take care of him."

Dutifully, our co-workers retreat back toward the hut, each of them casting one last longing look back at Gus before entering the building.

Gus bends down and lifts Jolly, slinging him over his shoulder effortlessly.

We begin walking toward the Well of Purity.

"Did you ever think to just ask him to throw you in the well?" Gus says.

"No. You know how he is about that thing. He never would have done it."

"I mean because, you know, technically, he's still not really throwing you into the well. If anything, you're throwing him into the well and going along for the ride. So, I guess what I'm saying is, what if the well still doesn't let you in?"

"Back to the drawing board. I'm trying to think positive. You're shitting on it."

"I just don't want you getting your hopes up. Have you gone to the doctor about the rash?"

"No."

"They could probably find out what's wrong with you."

"It's not about the rash. The rash is just a manifestation of everything else."

"Okay. I'm just saying . . . maybe it would be a start."

"This is where it starts." I point to the well ahead of us. "And finishes."

I want a Before and After like Gus. I want a Before and After where the After is better than the Before, not just an even shittier, more desperate version of the Before.

We reach the well.

"Well," Gus says, "here we are. Here we are, well. How do you wanna go about doing this?"

"I'll sit on the ledge. You can put him on my lap."

I sit on the ledge of the well. I lean back and peer down into it, smelling the scent of the cool, earthy water rising from it.

Gus places Jolly on my lap and I feel like a demented Santa Claus who throws children into wells.

"Wait," I say, reaching into my pants and extracting my phone. I hand it to Gus.

"Good luck," he says.

I take a deep breath and lean back.

I do not fall.

I do not plunge or plummet or drop.

What I do is lose my grip on Dr. Jolly as he shifts awkwardly, sending him into the well.

There's a loud splash and part of me hopes the chill of the water will be like a smelling salt bringing him back to consciousness.

The next thing I know I'm flying through the air, crashing to the ground and skidding along the grass.

I lie there for a moment, winded.

I try to take stock of myself.

I didn't hit my head. It doesn't feel like anything is broken. Other than the burns from sliding along the grass, I'm not really in a lot of pain.

I get to my feet and make my way over to Gus, who's staring down into the well.

"Plan B," I say.

"What's Plan B? Do you think he's going to be okay?"

"He'll be fine. Plan B is that *you* attempt to throw me into the well."

"Okay."

"Think about it. Clearly the magic has rubbed off on you. The world has opened up. Why wouldn't the well?"

"I said okay. We should probably do it now. I don't think it's good for him to be in there too long."

I collapse onto the grass and pretend to be dead. I think, if this worked for Gus, maybe it's part of it.

"What are you doing?" Gus says.

"Role playing."

He sighs and reaches down. He grabs me under the arms and lifts me up, propping me on the edge of the well and letting me go.

Again, I do not fall.

I do not plunge or plummet or drop.

Instead, I brace myself for what comes next.

This time I'm flung even farther and I'm pretty sure I break a couple of ribs on the landing.

I lie, breathing painfully and staring up at the summer clouds floating across the blue sky.

I tell myself I'm not going to cry.

I see Gus looking down at me.

"I'm a failure," I say.

"We should probably go," he says.

"Are we just going to leave him in there?"

"There's nothing we can do. I tried to jump in too. Couldn't. The only difference was that it didn't throw me."

I wonder if Dr. Jolly is going to die in there. I wonder if I should have Gus bludgeon me into unconsciousness. Maybe if Jolly were to rise from the well and find me in such a state, he would throw me in to resuscitate me, as he did Gus. It would be an even more accurate recreation of that night.

Gus offers a hand and helps me to my feet.

On the way to the parking lot, on the way to the truck, Gus says, "I'm sorry, man."

27
Coyote

I'M STANDING ON the sidewalk in front of the house, the yard bathed in the overly bright porchlight, staring at ... I don't know what I'm staring at, at first. I notice the grass in the yard is really long but, beyond that, it looks like the front of the Monarch's car is buried in the house. I never realized how small these houses are. Or maybe how big the Monarch's car actually is.

He had told me he couldn't drive it because the tires were all flat. Same situation as me. Looking at the tires now, they're not all flat.

But they are all different sizes.

This, I imagine, coupled with his constant state of inebriation, is what propelled the car into my house.

"I'm real sorry," he says.

It would startle me if I weren't in a state of near catatonia. The last few hours have been a blur. I choked off my emotions and disappeared within myself. After we'd left work, Gus took me to Easy J's where we ate in silence. Then he'd driven me home, me choking back tears the entire time, and driven away before either one of us had noticed the car in my house.

"It's just stuff." My voice sounds hollow and far away. The landlord will probably be ecstatic to hear about this. These houses are so cheap it's probably considered totaled, or demolished, or whatever you call houses that are beyond repair.

"Well . . ." The Monarch lights a cigarette.

"Not Alice."

I don't see how it's possible. She was usually in the bedroom fucking other people, well away from the destructive path of the Monarch's car.

"She was settin on the couch, I guess."

"Is she . . .?"

"Fraid so." He puts a hand on my shoulder. "Don't worry though. I didn't do nothin to her body."

I take my keys from my pocket and walk toward the house, wondering if I should unlock the front door or just crawl in around the Monarch's car.

I use the front door.

Walking in, I look to my left at the crumpled front of the Monarch's car and the pile of house debris soaking up the blood from a body that has been removed.

Not just a body.

Alice.

I didn't even like her very much, maybe even hated her, and had still managed to fail her completely. I couldn't even manage to keep her alive. Couldn't even do that one relatively simple thing.

This day suddenly seems way too long.

I wander into the bedroom and collapse onto the bed.

I haven't been home for three days so I don't even know if this took place today or not.

I pull the covers up around me and breathe in the scent of Alice and who knows how many guys.

I wonder if her purse full of money is still in the closet and immediately hate myself for the thought. But then I immediately tell myself I'm probably not going to go to her funeral.

119

Mentally exhausted, I drift off.

And wake up to a coyote crouched beside the bed.

Once I take a moment to clear the sleep from my brain, I'm a little scared, but the coyote doesn't seem to be particularly hostile. There is no snarling or baring of teeth. He's just sitting there panting, his tongue hanging out of his mouth like the mangy feral dog he is.

"What do you want?"

He shuffles a little closer, still resting on his haunches, licks my face, and springs to all fours. He leans his head back over his shoulder.

"You want me to get up?"

Of course he doesn't answer me. He's a coyote.

"Fine. I'll get up."

I pull myself out of the bed, try to ignore the aches and pains. It's still dark outside. I grab my phone from the floor and bring the screen to life. It's 5:23 a.m.

The coyote pads off into the living room.

I follow him.

He exits the house via a small gap between the window frame and the Monarch's car.

I use the front door.

I step outside. The neighborhood seems eerily quiet and I imagine the coyote slipping into the houses and killing everyone in their sleep. Even the nearby highway sounds hushed and far away. The air is rich with honeysuckle and moisture. The trees and surrounding lawns have a velvety look from dewfall or a recent rain.

"Okay," I say. "I'll follow you."

The coyote walks through the overgrown lawn and pauses when he reaches the sidewalk. I catch up to him and begin walking away from the dead end in front of the house.

"I hope you're not taking me to the Monarch's."

He's not. He walks up a block and turns to his left. I continue following him.

On this street the houses are even smaller and closer together. No driveways. The street is lined on both sides with cheap cars and over-sized trucks. Nearly every house has either a 'No Trespassing' sign, a sign for a security company, or a 'Beware of Dog' sign. Sometimes all three. What are these people trying to protect? What treasures lie in their tiny, faltering, mold-infested homes?

The coyote continues moving swiftly and confidently up the incline of the sidewalk, through the deep purple of the pre-dawn.

A few of the houses we pass have a single inside light on and I imagine some bedraggled blue collar guy sitting at a cheap kitchen table and smoking a cheap cigarette while the morning coffee brews, waiting to be put in a travel mug and used as a weak defense against the cold reality of a mild hangover and yet another day that's probably going to be a lot like the day before. It's a life I opted out of, if only slightly, but it seems almost romantic to me now.

I begin thinking of my early morning stroll as a guided tour of regret.

I had just accepted failure before Gus fell in the well. And then, once again, after seeing Gus's transformation, I'd thought there was some easy solution to my problems. Some way of tricking failure and, if not finding happiness, at least lessening the degree of misery.

But that was never meant for me.

I make a pact with myself to never try again.

At this point, it's just getting embarrassing.

Nevertheless, I continue following the coyote. I want to think he's taking me to some secret, magical location where everything makes sense. I would probably be just as happy if he were taking me back to his pack, where they would fall upon me and devour me, consuming all shreds of my existence so I could just blink out, leaving everyone around me to wonder what had happened to me for, like, two minutes.

Instead the coyote just leads me to a payphone in front of the Kroger and I think, "This is not very magical." I don't say it aloud because the payphone is by a bus stop and there are already a few mean looking people huddled around it, smoking cigarettes and angrily punching things into their phones. This has to be one of the last payphones on the planet. It looks anachronistic.

The grocery store across the parking lot hasn't opened yet, but there is already a line of people forming at the walk-up pharmacy window.

Sirens roar from the highway, startling me. The coyote belts out a howl and darts back the way we came. I imagine him living in the nature preserve behind the house, stalking the bike path and sustaining himself on the corpses of OD victims.

The payphone rings.

Of course it does.

I pick it up.

"Hello," I say.

There is no response.

I imagine the woman on the line. Of course I know who it is. I know who I want it to be. I've just been deluding myself.

I think of one of the first times I was with Callie. She pointed to one of her many tattoos and said, "I got this one–" and I cut her off because I didn't want to know. Not at the time. I wanted to make up my own story about it. I wanted it to be mysterious.

I imagine the person on the other end of the line sitting in a silenced tour bus, cutting through the still dark cornfields of Kansas.

I don't just imagine it.

I want it.

I want it to be true so much.

I lower my head and place the phone back in its stainless steel cradle.

I should have said something.

Maybe that's all she was waiting for. Waiting for me to say, "I miss you."

28
The Poet

SURPRISINGLY, GUS IS at work today. Probably for the same reason I am. We both want to find out if Dr. Jolly is there or if we are murderers. Jolly hasn't shown up by lunch and I think we probably need to explore our options. We go to Easy J's.

"If I was resurrected from the well, there's no way Jolly died down there," Gus says. "It's like *his* well."

"Did you ask anybody if they'd seen him?"

"No. I thought that would sound suspicious."

I sneeze, still recovering from the ride in with Diane Marbles, and give myself a vigorous scratchdown.

"Dude, you really need to get that looked at. You look like shit."

"Stop telling me that. You know I don't have the money. Especially now that I only have the one income and need to look for a place to live."

I float this last thing out there, leaving it hanging in the air.

"Oh, c'mon, Alice didn't pay for anything. She was more of a drain than an asset."

I think about defending her and decide I don't have the energy. Plus hearing her commodified like that—from Gus, of all people—hurts some infrequently thought about part of my soul.

"Still, that doesn't change the fact that I need to find a place to live."
I put it out there again. "The landlord was coming by the house today
to assess the situation. I'd be surprised if he ever lets me back in. Basically one side of the house is now a hole."

"Didn't you say Alice left some money behind?"

"She did, but I donated half to her funeral costs and the rest isn't going to last very long if I have to stay at a motel." A more veiled hint, but
still putting it out there nevertheless. "Actually, her family is probably
where all of it should have gone. It's more like I turned over half for
the funeral and donated the rest to myself, which is a nicer way of saying I stole it."

Gus scoffs. "Dude, it probably didn't come close to what you'd
spent on her since she moved in."

Our favorite waitress, Maybelline—the one with the lazy eye—stands
beside the table, ready to take our order.

"One check or separate?" she asks.

"One's fine," Gus says.

"I never know with you two. On again, off again, huh?" she smiles.

I'm surprised she still remembers this. The first time we'd ever had
her as a server, she'd put us on one check. I always just assumed this
was because it was easier. Gus, however, more than a little inebriated
at the time, asked if she thought we were gay and then explained the
test to her. Whenever the server asked about separate checks, we assumed that meant they thought we weren't gay. Whenever they didn't
bother to ask, we assumed they thought we were. I'm sure men and
women thought the same thing about the plutonic versus romantic
thing.

Gus gives her his order.

I order chicken and waffles and get really excited.

"Some places don't even split checks," Gus says. "They just make
you do it at the table, like we're all math wizards or something."

Gus points at my red barnacled hand resting on the table.

124

"Tarot swears it's gluten," he says.

I roll my eyes. "That sounds pretty much imaginary. Is Tarot a doctor?"

"No, but she's into the healthy eating, organic whole foods bullshit. She got second opinions when you were at our party. Resounding conclusion: gluten."

"Second opinions?"

"Yeah. When you were lying out in the yard. We all examined you."

"That's . . . really embarrassing."

"It was with love."

"Speaking of which, do you think I'd be able to stay with you for a while?" The hinting hasn't worked.

The length of his delay shocks me. But before he can answer, I get it. He's afraid my failure will rub off. Things have been going well for Gus. Better and better, actually. And during this cushy period of his life, he's watched me develop a rash, have a psychopath unleashed against me, have a car driven into my house, bury a girlfriend, and possibly drag him into being an accomplice to murder. This last thing makes me relax a little. If Gus is involved in any way whatsoever, there is no way Dr. Jolly is dead.

"Never mind," I say. "I get it."

I secretly hope Gus will say something like, "Of course you can stay with us, man. Don't be stupid."

But he doesn't. He looks slightly relieved and says, "You know I'd love to have you, man. But with Fee and so many other people coming and going, we've got quite the houseful most nights."

Wow. Not even the invitation for a couple of nights. I probably shouldn't have passed out in their backyard. That's always poor form. I just didn't think it would matter with Gus. And it wouldn't have mattered with the old Gus. But this is the new Gus, the After Gus.

"You've got your dad's place, right?"

Ouch. This would seem like a less bonkers suggestion if he'd never met the man.

"I'll let Tarot put me on a strictly gluten-free diet or whatever."

There. Who can resist the idea of practical martyrdom? I'm pledging to throw myself in their hands. Thus, if he says no, my fate ultimately rests on him.

He doesn't take the bait. "You don't really have to live with us for her to do that. You can probably just look on the internet."

"I'm sure I'd find some way to fuck it up."

Maybelline comes back with our food.

"You boys need to cheer up," she says.

Even she notices I've made things awkward.

"Can I come and live with you, Maybelline? My best friend is too busy with his new friends to be accommodating."

She laughs a little and shoos me away with a bony hand.

"You wouldn't want that, hon. I'm livin in my car in the parkin lot." Then she leans in closer and whispers, "I even got to wash up in the employee restroom. Truckers used to treat me real nice, but not no more. Everyone's flat broke. Let me know if y'all need anything else."

She turns and heads back toward the kitchen.

We eat in silence. I stare at my food before putting it into my mouth, wondering if it's killing me. Gus types messages into his phone. I want to think he's lobbying Tarot on my behalf but know he's probably just sexting one of her young fair maiden friends. I imagine him roleplaying cult sex with Fee and shudder.

I find a group of people sitting a couple tables away to focus on. There's a rough looking man and two teenage girls. It's probably some trucker dad, in the area to take his daughters to lunch or something. Instead I imagine him as a working class poet with a name like Chuck Eldridge or something. Something masculine but still slightly distinguished sounding. He's a small press guy, but widely respected. He lives in a tiny cinderblock house by a gravel pit overlooking Dayton. It's slightly dangerous and a little scary, but the wildness is what makes it intoxicating. Like his writing. These girls are his acolytes, two of many who make the journey of hundreds of miles just to see how he lives and hope some of his magic poetry wears off on them. When they get up to go, I notice he can't even straighten up all the way. I imagine this is part of it. Imagine him saying, "A poet doesn't work, ladies. That's why I removed several vertebrae just to go on disability. We have to make sacrifices for art." And before the bill is even paid, they're contemplating doing the same thing. They'll go back to his house, get blind drunk, and take turns hitting each other in the spine with metal rods while the poet dances around a trash fire and howls at the moon.

I wonder if I should try for disability, what with the rash and the probably broken ribs and undiagnosed mental illness.

We finish our lunch and I feel moderately queasy and write it off to not having had that big a meal in a long time.

Gus pays.

We head back to work.

Dr. Jolly is there.

Of course he is.

The office is abuzz with the latest news.

The even bigger windfall that Dr. Jolly has anticipated has finally happened. The Point, the biggest company in the world, has bought Dr. Jolly's Godwater, effective immediately. We all get to work twice as many hours at half the pay and no benefits, even though the Point owns most of the hospitals in the area and is one of the leading pharmaceutical manufacturers.

Well, everyone except Gus.

He gets a very generous severance package and will never have to work again.

Then Dr. Jolly tells us he's moving to Santa Cruz, California, and isn't planning on coming back.

We get in Gus's truck and he says, "Man, this sucks."

"For me," I say.

"Well . . . yeah."

29
This Installment Plan Isn't Working

GUS DROPS ME off in the driveway. I ask if he wants to come in and hang out for a bit but he says he doesn't want to because Dayton makes him nervous.

I gingerly get out of his truck and watch him back out onto the street because I'm in absolutely no hurry to go inside the house. His reverse lights illuminate my car. I've gotten so used to it being parked in the same place that I've stopped noticing it.

I only really notice it now because Bart's big black truck is parked on top of it. I don't even really see how this is possible except Bart's truck is huge and my car is very small.

The driver's side door to his truck pops open and he hops out just as Gus speeds away.

I hear the creaking door of Mapes's house open and he struggles down his porch steps with his girth and two of his little yapping dogs.

"Go back inside, old man," Bart says to him.

He doesn't realize Mapes is only about half-there mentally, if that. Mapes just stares vacantly, Bart's ire setting the little dogs to yipping.

I continue toward the house.

"I've come for the second installment," Bart says.

"I don't have it," I say without thinking. That isn't exactly true. I do have it. From Alice's stash. But I'm going to need it for other things like food and possibly a place to live.

"Then I'm going to have to give you a beating," he says.

My ribs still hurt from the beating the well gave me.

"A beating is not going to give me a greater ability to make money," I say. Then I point to my car. "Much like removing my only mode of transportation didn't give me the ability to make money. I'd probably have it to give you if I hadn't spent so much on the bus and rideshares."

"Not my problem," Bart says. "I'm just doing a job."

"Tell Jen to go fuck herself."

"It's not for Jen. It's for Charles."

Even the kid's beloved uncle doesn't know his fucking name.

"If you cared so much then you might get his name right. It's Charle. Not Charles."

"That's what I fuckin said. Don't make fun of me."

I sigh and stand there. I have to bend over slightly in order to breathe.

"Okay," I say. "Get it over with. Sure hope this rash isn't contagious."

But I'm not sure Bart knows what 'contagious' means.

He moves in and quickly beats me to the ground before kicking me over to the far side of the driveway.

I guess it hurts, and it's certainly embarrassing, but now I just feel mostly numb.

He kicks until he's panting and exhausted.

I lie there with my arms pulled around my head, half hoping I just pass out and wake up in a hospital somewhere.

Once finished, he spits on the back of my head and says, "Get that money, motherfucker."

I hear his truck start up and roll over.

One of Mapes's dogs hikes his leg and unleashes a torrent of piss onto the side of my face. Then it squats down and shits right next to me.

"Mapes, you old retard, get them things in the house."

It's the Monarch, reaching down and helping me to my feet.

I'm pretty sure I need medical attention.

He walks me toward the house. My vision is blurred and I'm grateful the Monarch is there to guide me.

He pulls a piece of paper from the door and says, "You seen this?"

I shake my head.

"It says these premises have been condemned and occupancy of this property is prohibited. You think them boys have been up to their pranks again?"

"No," I rasp. "I'm pretty sure this is real."

"Where ya gonna go?"

I point to the door. "In there."

"You can stay at my place," he says.

"I don't want to walk that far."

"Suit yourself then." He hands me his half-drank can of beer. I don't know where he produced it from until I remember the cup holder around his waist. "Might need this."

I take it and practically fall through the front door. I think I close it behind me but maybe I don't. I collapse onto the floor and fall asleep or possibly enter a mild coma.

30
Spent

"COME ON. Get up."

The voice is very authoritative. The shoe that I open my eyes far enough to see, the shoe nudging me into consciousness, is highly polished and very black. I reach out to rub its shiny surface.

"Don't touch the shoes, you filthy creep."

But the shoe was touching me, I think.

"Give me a second," I say.

"We don't have a second. We've got more important things to do. We got a call. We've got to escort you off the premises. Unless you want us to take you in for trespassing."

"I signed a lease." It sounds useless.

"You'll have to take that up with the landlord. The city says no one's supposed to be in here."

I pull myself up onto my hands and knees and manage to straighten up and force myself woozily to my feet.

There are two cops standing just inside the doorway to the house.

"You been drinkin?" the second cop says, kicking over the half-empty can of beer.

"No," I say. "That was the Monarch's."

"He's probably a schizo," the first cop says. "Let's just get him out of here."

They each grab one of my arms and I pull my feet off the ground. Not because I don't want to leave the house but because it's what people on cop shows always do and I don't know when I'll have another chance. At this point, my goals in life have diminished to about that extent.

I briefly panic about leaving the money behind but reassure myself I can get back in because I have the key. I'll just wait until they're gone.

"Don't let us catch you back here again," the first cop says.

The second cop nods toward the car and says, "That the piece of shit Bart mentioned?"

"Yeah," the first cop says.

"We'll get a tow truck out here for it."

"This your car?" the first cop asks.

"Nope," I lie.

"Better hope not," he says. "I could write five different tickets for five different things right now."

The second cop checks his watch. "We gotta go."

"We're gonna go get some free pussy and find a black guy to beat up on. It's a big morning."

I stand there until they drive away, not really knowing what to do. I reach into my pocket to grab my keys and notice my pants feel weird. I pull the waistband out and peer down, half expecting to see that the rash has mutated even further. Instead, I find Alice's money. I must have stuffed it all down my pants sometime during my coma.

I just leave it there.

I pull out my phone and shamble along the sidewalk.

There are a couple of other lone men shambling along the sidewalk on the other side of the street. I've seen people like this regularly since moving back to Dayton and assumed they were all some form of drug addict. Now I see them differently. Maybe they're people like me.

What kind of person is that?

A loser.

A failure.

People who've spent their arsenal and, having never hit the target, just given up.

I type 'Team Klaus' into the search bar.

Hadn't that Mason guy mentioned something about them being in the area?

What was I going to do if they were?

My life has felt like a nightmare ever since leaving Callie.

I turn and look back at the house, the Monarch's car still lodged in the front of it. I look at my own car, destroyed, a pile of metal shit on the curb.

If I could turn my back on all of my dreams, why couldn't I turn my back on the nightmares too?

31
On The Road With Team Klaus

"WHAT IF IT'S sold out?" Gus asks.

"This isn't Europe, dude. There's no way it's going to sell out."

Gus maneuvers his large truck into a narrow parking space in the Oregon District.

We get out of the truck and light cigarettes because smoking is great and we don't know how long the line at the club is going to be. It's probably not really a club. More like a bar. 'Venue' is probably the most generous term.

The night is warm and breezy, the sun just now disappearing from the sky. It's around nine and, even though that's when the doors open, I know we're probably here way too early. Team Klaus rarely performs before midnight unless it's at some kind of private event. Although they have gotten a little older. Maybe they've changed.

"So," Gus says, "it's really been two years since you've seen her, huh?"

"Yep."

"No contact even?"

I think about the mysterious calls I get. Is this considered contact? Are they even from Callie?

"Nope," I say.

We stop at the back of the line. It's only about fifteen people deep. Once we stop moving and are forced to stand still, I have to bend over a little to feel remotely comfortable. It feels like my insides are bruised. The only good thing about the beatings received from the well and Bart is that the intense, almost never-ending pain has taken my mind off the rash.

A homeless man with a massive growth on his lower lip shuffles up to us.

"Gotta smoke?"

"Sure, man." Gus pulls the pack from his pocket and hands the guy two.

"Got a phone I can use?"

"Sorry, man." We both have phones but both feel this is asking too much.

"Fuck you then!" the guy says. "I ain't got nobody to call no way." Then he shuffles a little down the sidewalk to begin the exact same encounter with someone else.

"Even the homeless people in Dayton are assholes," Gus says.

As we draw closer to the door, I notice Team Klaus's opening act is a band called The Skelebongs.

"Man," I say, "I've been waiting a long time to see The Skelebongs."

Gus smiles a little and says, "Hey, they're from Twin Springs. They were at my party the other night."

"I guess I won't make fun of them then," I sigh.

"You can," Gus says. "If it makes you feel better, I guess."

But it won't. Not now. It's this final thing that makes me realize I've lost Gus as a best friend. There would have been a time when trading jabs about a band called The Skelebongs would have been the secondary focus of our evening, running closely behind the main reason we were there. And if the main event turned out to be a dud, we wouldn't have been able to talk about anything but The Skelebongs. I'm not really sure if Gus has changed or if I'm just an immature dick.

Gus pays for both of us and we enter the venue. There are some tables lining a mostly open floor, a small stage pushed into a corner in front of a large plate glass window.

We go to the bar and order beers and take them out to the patio so we can resume smoking. Thank god for party patios. Before walking out, I glance around to see if I can spot Callie. I don't. And I'm not sure if I'm ready to see her yet or not. I know I won't see her on the smoking patio. There are a lot of bands that hang out drinking and smoking before they go on. Team Klaus is not such a band. I guess they really can't be if they want to preserve their mystery. Especially not if they want people to keep thinking they're guys.

I find an empty table with a couple of chairs on the patio.

"I think I need to sit down," I say.

Even when I'm standing, it feels like my body is trying to assume some kind of sitting position.

We sit down and Gus pulls out his phone and says, "I'm gonna see if I can get some more people here."

"I'm going to think about all the horrible turns my life has taken," I reply.

It wasn't that the end of things with Callie was the beginning of all the horribleness. It was just that my time with her was like a blissful hiatus from the horribleness. It was my fault it ended. As of right now, it is the single biggest regret of my life.

They were on a tour of the West Coast. It started in Idaho and made its way over to Washington, Oregon, and down through several cities in California. They played to increasingly large crowds and it was to culminate with three nights in L.A., where the goal was to draw some attention from a certain respectable indie label with huge distribution that had been putting out exactly the stuff they had been making. Everything was going well. Everything was working out exactly like the band wanted it to.

Apparently I was deathly afraid of even other people's success.

Intimacy on the road was difficult for Callie and me. It was rare we had a moment to ourselves. And when we did she was either too anxious about the show she was going to perform or too tired from the show they'd just performed to really be present. The noise and the travel were too much for me to focus on writing. It was a struggle to even concentrate on reading a book. The anxiety would take hold and my mind would go to dark places. The literal definition of 'anxiety' is probably 'the state of being anxious.' I would define it as simply exploring the worst-case scenario of any given situation. I was an expert at that. That was one thing I had never failed at.

Rachel was Blue Klaus's little sister. She was 'taking a break' from college, helping Team Klaus to sell merchandise and get up and on the road in the morning. I'd never met her before that tour. We ended up spending a lot of time together. We talked. Not about anything serious. I never got the impression either one of us had any feelings for each other at all, except as chummy acquaintances. In other words, there was nothing in me that warned me to stay away from her. Not that she was predatory. Just a lonely, sheltered girl with hormones bouncing to the moon and back.

It was the second to last night in L.A. I had drunk way more than I had any previous night, ramping up before the last show in two days and the inevitable come down van ride across the lonely middle of the country before ending up back in Ohio to settle into relative normalcy, something I longed for but something that seemed impossibly far off.

I was headed down a long hallway to the restrooms. Rachel was on her way back.

"Hey," she said, approaching me. "I know you."

Then she pointed at me, moved in closer.

I gave her a dubious, squint-eyed look, as though I was trying to figure out who she was.

And we moved closer and closer, our eyes locking, neither one of us stopping.

I knew what was going to happen and knew it was wrong. Knew I didn't even want it to happen. And there was that stupid, self-sabotaging part of my brain that said, "Why not?"

Everything had been working out for Team Klaus, which meant they would end up getting signed to the label they wanted and would have to come back here to record and would have to embark on bigger, longer tours, and I'd be left behind. I was holding Callie back.

I didn't stop mine and Rachel's imminent collision. We kissed sloppily and got moderately handsy with one another. The whole thing lasted a minute at most.

The immediate regret was sobering.

I pushed her away and said, "I can't. You understand? I really have to pee."

She made a dejected face and slumped back against the wall.

I peed and told myself if she was still in the hall when I opened the door that I would stay in the restroom and hide from her.

When I opened the door to the restroom she was gone.

But the regret was still there.

I couldn't not tell Callie this had happened. I could justify not telling her until we returned home because it would sound considerate, like I didn't want to throw a pall over their last couple of shows. But, eventually, I would have to tell her. I would have to break her heart, even if it didn't result in us breaking up. I would have to watch whatever faith and trust she had in me vanish like I'd watched most people's expectations in me vanish.

I took the easy way out. Well, the easiest way out for the time being. I didn't think what I was doing at the time would throw a shadow over the rest of my life.

I left the club and took a cab to a Greyhound station, took the Greyhound to an Amtrak station, took the train back to Ohio, and called Gus to pick me up from the station.

We never talked about what I did. When we got back to the apartment, I loaded my few meager possessions into Gus's truck and he drove me to my dad's house, where I slept in the garage and went to work, where I eventually met Alice.

Other than a few texts from that fateful night asking me where I was, Callie had never contacted me.

I'd never contacted her.

I wondered if Rachel had ever told her what had happened.

I sit at the table and smoke and drink and watch Gus operate his phone like a sorceror. It's like he sends a text and poof—a whole other group of people shows up. The place is packed in under an hour.

I slide off my chair and struggle to straighten up.

"Let's go, man," I say.

"Go?" Gus says, his eyebrows raised.

"Yeah."

"You want to leave?"

"Yes." I'm a little curt. It sounds a little like a hiss.

"I can probably get you back there if you want to see her."

Part of me does want to see her, just to say I'm sorry. But I don't want her to see me. And I realize how selfish it was to come to this thing, to think she wants to see me in any way. The way I treated her doesn't really deserve a second chance. And it would just end in failure anyway. Maybe that's why my life has always been shit. I'm unable to accept something broken and mended. I have to walk away and find something fresh and new. But the doors I find opening onto new lives are now closing in my face.

"Look at me," I say. "I'm a fucking disease. She doesn't want to see me."

Gus crushes out his cigarette, as close to anger as I've seen him in a really long time.

"Okay, man. Where you want to go?"

Translation: "Where do you want me to take you that isn't my place?"

"Just take me to my dad's," I say.

"All right then. Let's go. I'm coming back. I'm not gonna leave my bros hanging."

32
Noman's Land

"So what the heck happened to you?" Dad says.

We're sitting around the breakfast table. I spent last night in one of their deck chairs because all the lights were off when Gus dropped me off and I didn't want to knock on the door or ring the bell because I was afraid Malinda would answer it and she makes me kind of nervous.

Dad's question is so general I don't answer him right away. Is he asking about the rash? The black eyes? The leaning stoop? Why I ended up on his patio? My entire life up to this point? I decide to go with that one.

"Well," I say, "first I was born and then ... it's all been kind of downhill from there."

"Don't be a smartass. That ain't what I meant. You're mentally deficient. We get it. It looks like you got beat up."

"Um, yeah. That was a couple days ago. I got jumped."

"Why the hell anyone would live in Dayton—especially without owning a gun—is just friggin beyond me."

"Well, I don't live there anymore."

This takes him by surprise. He sets down his piece of toast because if he doesn't he knows I'll notice the rage-tremble his hand develops.

He clears his throat. "I hope you don't think you're movin back here."

"Just for a few nights."

"I guess that girl of yours finally got tired of you, huh?"

I think about answering truthfully and decide he's not worth the effort.

"You could say that," I say, and think, *So tired of me she died.*

Trish, already heavily medicated, takes a sip of her Bloody Mary and says, "I think it'd be great to have you around. I'm sure Malinda would like the company, wouldn't you?"

It pains me to look at the girl, sitting with her legs pulled up in the chair, her sleeping shorts truncating just below her vagina, a narrow band between her legs, her ripe nipples taut against the fabric of her tank top. She's not wearing any make-up yet and looks way less trashy than usual. Looking at her in this way just confirms that my brain is rotting.

She rolls her eyes and says, "Whatever."

And even though I'm a forty-year-old man, I'm now in the same position as this teen girl. Actually a far worse position. She probably has a shred of optimism left in her.

I'm afraid Dad's gong to grill me about my plans but Trish picks up the remote and turns the TV on. It's a show about obese hoarders and I realize entertainment hasn't changed much over the years. We're still just watching freak shows at the carnival. The show is one of the most depressing things I've watched and it makes me feel better about my life. Maybe that's why these things exist.

I gesture to the TV and say, "What? Couldn't find a good holocaust documentary."

Nobody answers me.

After breakfast I spend the next several hours wandering around the house in a depressed stupor and trying not to ogle Malinda. In an effort to stop I go to the bathroom and stream some internet porn on my phone. It hurts to come and the experience leaves my penis stinging and bleeding slightly. I really need to go to the doctor. And it doesn't help things with Malinda. It makes them worse. Porn is one thing but porn is not an actual female. You can't touch it. It has no mass, no smell.

I think about rejoining MyFace.

I think about taking a walk.

I think about reading a book or listening to some music on my phone.

Instead I just lie in the middle of the living room floor and stare up at the ceiling until Dad nudges me with his foot and says, "Let's go down to the shooting range."

"I'd prefer to just lie here."

"Come on," he says, nudging me a little harder. It's really more like a kick.

I painfully stand up, wincing.

"Want me to get you some Tylenol?" Trish sounds dazed and faraway. "I probably have something stronger."

"What's the point?"

I follow Dad to the door of the basement shooting range.

"I don't want to shoot any guns," I say.

He turns his head over his shoulder and says in a soft voice I don't think I've ever heard him use, "I know. I just want to talk to you."

For some reason, this fills me with more dread than the idea of playing with lethal weapons.

The basement is cool and mostly gray. Fluorescent lights buzz overhead. A paper target hangs at the far end in a way that strikes me as ghoulish. Actually, the whole shooting range seems mind numbingly depressing. Sterile and smelling of machine oil and chemicals, I don't see how anyone can enjoy spending time down here.

I'm preparing myself for a heart-to-heart conversation with Dad. It's not something I want to have. It would be the first time ever.

"How much do you need to be gone by tonight?" he says. He's not looking at me. His eyes are focused longingly on the distant target and

I wonder why he doesn't just write 'Ryan' above its head.

I think about naming a price but that makes things too easy for him. I'm a shitty dad and I've paid for it practically every day of Charle's life. Why should my dad get off the hook so easily?

"Money's not really the problem. I have some. I just . . . I don't feel great, okay? I thought I could chill out here for a few days."

He scratches his chin and continues to avoid eye contact.

"That ain't a good idea," he says.

"Why? Trish seemed okay with it. Malinda doesn't seem to care about anything. So what's the problem?"

"It ain't up to them. I don't want you here. You're the problem."

I'm slightly stunned and find myself blinking away tears. While I'd always thought this was the case and it should have been refreshing to hear him actually say it, the words sting a lot more than I thought they would.

"I've got a . . . a good thing here. I've worked hard for it. I deserve it. You're gonna mess it up if you stick around. I don't really know what's been goin on with you since you been on your own but remember when you was a teenager? You and Jen and Gus always hangin out and havin fun? I feel a little bit like that now. It's how I want to spend my last years. Havin fun. Not worryin about much. Sometimes Malinda can be a mouthy little bitch, but Trish takes care of that. Malinda ain't my problem. Never will be my problem. And Trish is always goin to take care of her cause she knows she's got a good thing here. She respects me. If you stay, you're my problem. And I've gone too long without problems to start dealing with em now. I guess I've just never liked you, Ryan. I wanted to. I tried. But I knowed you was different from the time you was little. I knowed we'd never get along. And it was true. Your mom always said it was cause we was too much alike. But that ain't true at all. We couldn't be more different. You're just a whiny spoiled brat who's never worked a day in his life. You want nice things, think you deserve some great life, but you ain't never been willin to work for em. You couldn't provide for Jen. Sure as hell ain't

143

providin for Charles now. I stopped askin myself when you was gonna grow up. So I guess that's the lesson for ya. Whether you want to hear it or not. Whether you want it to be true or not. You're an adult now. Your growed up. I wrote you a check for five thousand dollars. I'll give you the keys to the old work truck and that's it from me. I ain't got nothin else to give ya."

This is probably as much as I've heard my dad say my entire adult life, possibly ever. Like he'd been storing it all up. I want to talk back to him. I want to argue with him but I don't see a point in it. I've worked nearly every day of my adult life. So it wasn't a factory union job where I made four times as much money. I'd applied for those jobs and no one had hired me. I'd written about five books since getting out of high school and had worked my ass off trying to sell them to publishers or get representation from an agent. That was all in addition to working a day job. And trying to debate being an adult with a grown man who used the word 'growed' instead of 'grown' and had a twelve-year-old's fixation with guns seemed completely futile.

I think about saying "I don't need your money or your truck," even though it isn't true.

I don't want to say anything or maybe I'm too choked up to say anything.

"Wait a minute," he says, moving closer to me.

I stop.

"I, um, I got cancer. Just found out last week. I ain't told the girls yet. I just wanted to let you know cause you'll probably get it too." He pauses. "I hope you do. Soon."

I just turn and head back up the stairs, blinking away tears.

On my way through the living room, I cast one leering glance at Malinda, asleep on the couch, and head for the front door.

"You takin off?" Trish calls.

I don't answer her.

I step out into the humid air and check my phone at the end of the driveway.

I'm going to send Gus a text asking if he can pick me up when I notice I've received a text from Jen.

It's a photo of Charle. A booking photo from a police station. There's nothing accompanying it. In the photo, Charle is smiling. He's missing an ear. It's the first photo she's sent in about six years.

I text Gus: "Can you pick me up in Milltown? I really need to talk to you."

I walk aimlessly, guessing I'll pop into the first restaurant I come to so I can sit down and kill some time. I can't keep walking. It hurts too much.

I find a diner and take a spot at the counter, order some coffee. I fit in with all the decrepit old people littering the place. I entertain thoughts of my dad dying alone in a hospital and dismiss it. It makes me feel bad to think about him that way. Better not to think of him at all. I pull my phone out and look at the picture of Charle. The coffee comes and I leave it sitting untouched while I think about what I'm going to do. I guess I'll go to Dr. Jolly's tomorrow and beg to keep my job. I'll see if I can rent a room or an apartment in town. There's a cheap motel at the edge of Twin Springs. I can probably afford to stay there for a few nights. I keep thinking like this until my mind is just a muddied swamp and the thoughts kind of just go away. The waitress behind the counter is nice. She doesn't hassle me too much. Just periodically asks if she can get me anything and I tell her no thanks, not right now, and I wonder if she knows I'm on the brink of tears and figure she probably does. She sees a hundred faces a day and is probably better at knowing what's going on behind them than most psychologists.

Three hours later, Gus texts, "Still in Milltown?"

"Yep," I text, then give him the name of the diner.

"On my way," he texts back.

33
All Truth Is Painful

WE GO TO EASY J'S. The ride is silent save for the music coming from the truck's stereo.

It's nearly dark and we sit in a booth and watch the cars on the highway whip past in the gray dusk. Trucks come and go from the pumps, the entire restaurant trembling with a bass rumble. I have trouble sitting up straight and lean forward with my elbows on the table.

"So I might need to stay with you for a few days. Just a few days."

Gus takes a sip of his Coke and looks down at the table.

"I'm sorry, man. That's not possible."

"Why not?"

His answer is delayed. He plays with the wrapper to his straw.

"Everything okay with you and Tarot?" I ask, just to be saying something.

"Everything's fine." He pauses again, possibly trying to think of a lie or whether or not he should tell me the truth. "It's just . . ."

"I understand if you don't want me there. I'm a downer. I get it. I can stay at a motel or something. I've got a few bucks. Just thought it wouldn't hurt to ask."

"Callie's there," he says.

It's like a punch to the gut.

"What?" I cough out.

"Callie's there. She came back with us last night. I . . . I think she might move in for a while. Until they go on tour again."

A number of things streak through my brain. I had wanted to ask Gus about something, trying to convince myself what I wanted to ask him about wasn't possible. Now I just want to ask him about Callie. If I were a more egotistical person, I'd convince myself she went home with Gus in some roundabout way of getting in contact with me. In reality, I doubt she even asked about me. I imagine Gus approaching her at the show last night. I imagine her marveling at his transformation, suddenly enamored like everyone else. And I imagine him taking full advantage of that.

"I'm sorry," he says. "We were talking and I gave her a ride and . . . it just happened."

Again, I realize what he's saying and the reality of it doesn't shock me.

"You fucked her." I try to sound calm.

"It was Tarot's idea."

I pull out my phone.

"Jen sent me a picture of Charle," I say.

Gus seems momentarily confused at the change of subject and says, "Oh yeah? Let's see it."

I turn the phone to face him and slide it across the table.

I watch his expression drop.

He slides the phone back to me like it's about ready to explode.

"He's a . . . very handsome young man," Gus says.

"Yeah," I say. "Looks a little like you. A lot like you, actually."

Gus takes a sip of his Coke and rubs his perfectly sculpted, glowing face.

I don't say anything. Just keep watching him. I try to remain visibly calm but my insides are bubbling and popping so much it feels like my already compromised skin might burst open.

"What do you want me to say?" Gus says.

"I don't know. I don't think anything can make it better."

"It happened once," Gus says. "You were being a shit. We were both drunk and it just happened. We didn't tell you because we knew it would never happen again."

"That makes it worse." I pocket the phone and lean back in the booth. "Well, it looks like once was enough, huh?"

"She never told me," he says. "I swear. I barely ever even talked to her." And then, as if reading my mind, he says, "This doesn't mean I owe you anything, man. You got that?"

Maybelline comes over, looking too exhausted to even stand up straight.

"Everything okay? You boys look tense."

"Everything's great," I say.

"You ready to order?"

We give her our order. I specify that it's to be separated into two checks and she mutters, "Trouble in paradise."

Gus and I don't say anything else to each other.

When he drops me off at the motel, I'm not sure I'll ever see him again.

34
Later

Dr. Jolly's campus is only about a half hour's walk from the Starlighter Motel. I'm only able to afford staying at the motel because I mow the lawn on the weekends and pick up trash in the parking lot and man the front desk when I get back from Dr. Jolly's. Only Dr. Jolly's isn't Dr. Jolly's anymore. Now it's just called Godwater. Every day I have to cross picketers brandishing signs reading 'Keep Big Business Out of Twin Springs.' I couldn't agree with them more. I try to look apologetic but never say anything because they would just tell me I'm part of the problem. Which is true.

I go off gluten thinking, Why not? It feels like I'm living some other life anyway. This basically just means giving up all the remaining vaguely affordable things that give me a shred of joy—beer, pizza, junk food. The rash is still there, but it doesn't seem to itch as badly. Maybe I'm just telling myself that. I live on canned fruits, vegetables, and beans and tell myself it's healthier. But it's really just because I'm poor and forced to eat like a hobo.

About a week after moving into the motel, I walk into town, thinking I would go to Gus's and force some sort of resolution. But maybe it's just because I'm lonely. I stop on the sidewalk in front of his house because my phone rings.

Unknown number.

I think about answering it but glance toward Gus's house and see him, Callie, Tarot, and Fee sitting around the dinner table, talking animatedly and laughing. I can't help thinking I narrowly missed being a part of this. Some lingering shred of laughable optimism tells me it's not too late.

I press the 'ignore' icon and return the phone to my pocket. I go to a coffee shop and get an iced coffee, wonder when I'll be forced to give that up too.

Then I go back to the motel and pick up the trash in the parking lot and relieve Mr. Rangely at the front counter. I watch TV and doze on the sofa in the lobby. This now constitutes my nightly sleep. Nobody checks in that night so I get a lot of rest.

Mr. Rangely relieves me at six a.m.

"Supposed to get some bad storms later," he says.

"Huh," I say. "I should have watched the Weather Channel."

"Don't get stuck out in it."

"Doesn't matter."

I head out to the Godwater campus, wondering if Mr. Rangely is correct because the sky is clear and blue and there doesn't seem to be any humidity in the air.

At the Godwater campus, I no longer sit in a chair and fill glass bottles through a positively charged quartz faucet while listening to music. Everything's automated now. And earbuds are against safety regulations. The plastic bottles are set on a conveyor belt and filled with water that comes from some massive tank that appeared shortly after Jolly's departure. Many more people work there but, aside from the office sales team, nearly everyone just packs boxes and loads trucks.

The job used to be mildly irritating but quirky enough to be tolerable. Now it's just an unendurable slog.

That afternoon we gather on the loading docks and watch the wall of black roll toward us.

Something inside of me wakes up.

The pressure drops, the air cools down, and the breeze picks up, drying the sweat on my face.

Lightning streaks across the sky, some of it horizontally, from cloud to cloud, punctuated with fat bolts from sky to ground and bone rattling thunder.

It starts raining and the rest of my co-workers retreat into the building.

I stay out in it.

My clothes are soaked in a second and the wind feels like it's pulling me along. I let it take me. Around the building and out into the field behind the campus.

I let it take me all the way to the Well of Purity.

I climb up on the wall surrounding the well. The grass around it is overgrown and it looks sad and abandoned. It's raining so hard I can barely see anything and when the lightning flashes it's so bright it bleaches everything and leaves neon tremors in its wake. I stand on the low wall surrounding the well and raise my hands above my head, trying to make myself tall but knowing I'll never be tall enough.

I step off the wall, over the well.

I do not fall.

I do not plunge.

I do not plummet.

I do not drop.

I float.

Other **Atlatl Press** Books

Made in the USA
Columbia, SC
07 March 2018